Ernest Hemingway

◆

THE FIFTH
COLUMN

SCRIBNER

NEW YORK   LONDON   TORONTO   SYDNEY

SCRIBNER

A Division of Simon & Schuster, Inc.
1230 Avenue of the Americas
New York, NY 10020

First Scribner trade paperback edition May 2008

SCRIBNER and design are registered trademarks of The Gale Group, Inc.,
used under license by Simon & Schuster, Inc., the publisher of this work.

For information about special discounts for bulk purchases,
please contact Simon & Schuster Special Sales at 1-800-456-6798
or business@simonandschuster.com.

Text set in Sabon

Manufactured in the United States of America

1   3   5   7   9   10   8   6   4   2

Library of Congress Control Number: 70182369

ISBN-13: 978-1-4165-9493-2
ISBN-10: 1-4165-9493-0

THE FIFTH COLUMN received its first performance at the Mint Theater (Jonathan Bank, Artistic Director; Sherri Kotimsky, General Manager) in New York, N.Y., on February 26, 2008. It was directed by Jonathan Bank, the set design was by Vicki R. Davis, the costume design was by Clint Ramos, the lighting design was by Jeff Nellis, the sound design was by Jane Shaw, the properties were by Scott Brodsky, the dialect coach was Amy Stoller, the dramaturg was Juan Salas, the stage manager was Allison Deutsch, and the assistant stage manager was Jeff Meyers. The cast was as follows:

I.B. Soldier	John Patrick Hayden
Girl	Maria Parra
Dorothy Bridges	Heidi Armbruster
Robert Preston	Joe Hickey
Hotel Manager	Carlos Lopez
Philip Rawlings	Kelly AuCoin
Electrician	Ryan Duncan
Anita	Nicole Shalhoub
I.B. Soldier	Ned Noyes
Assault Guard	Ryan Duncan
Petra	Teresa Yenque
Wilkinson	Joe Rayome
Maid	Maria Parra
Killer	Ryan Duncan
Antonio	James Andreassi
Waiter	Ryan Duncan
Max	Ronald Guttman
Sentry	Ned Noyes
Aide	John Patrick Hayden
Civilian	Ryan Duncan
General	Joe Hickey
Signaller	Joe Rayome
Assault Guard	Joe Rayome

CHARACTERS

Two Girls
Two International
   Brigade Soldiers
Dorothy Bridges
Robert Preston
Manager
Philip Rawlings
Electrician
Anita [Moorish Tart]
First Comrade
Second Comrade
Two Assault Guards
Petra

Comrade Wilkinson
Maid
Killer
Antonio
Waiter
Rifle Comrade
Max
Two Sentries
Two Signallers
General [Large Officer]
Aide [Thin Officer]
Civilian

Production Note

Mint Theater Company's Premiere production of *The Fifth Column* used thirteen actors. Some characters specified in the script were eliminated but no lines were cut to accommodate those changes. For example, only one SENTRY, one SIGNALLER, and one ASSAULT GUARD were used. A few actors played multiple roles: PRESTON doubled as the GENERAL, the ELECTRICIAN as the CIVILIAN, etc., but certain characters were also combined. The International Brigade SOLDIERS in Act One, Scene One were the same as the International Brigade COMRADES in Act One, Scene Three (the Soldier with the GIRL was not the same Soldier who is later interrogated by Antonio—and after that interrogation the Soldier in I.B. uniform was never seen again).

N.B. This text preserves the original character tags from the first published edition of the play; for example, Anita is MOORISH TART in her first scene and ANITA the next time we see her; and the LARGE OFFICER and THIN OFFICER become GENERAL and AIDE and so on.

PROPERTY LIST

Furniture

Room 109 bed
Room 109 bed dressing
Room 109 bed table
Room 110 bed
Room 110 bed dressing
Room 110 bed table
Room 109 desk
Room 109 desk chair
Room 110 table
Room 110 chair
Wardrobe/armoire
Seguridad Headquarters
   table
Seguridad Headquarters
   chairs
Chicotes Bar table
2 Chicotes Bar chairs
Observation post table
Observation post chairs

Weapons

2 rifles
Pistol
Pistol
Automatic rifle
Mauser pistol
Rifle
Automatic rifle
Hand grenade

Props

Hanging sign
Thumbtacks
Nail file
Hair brush
Room 109 lamp
Room 109 telephone
Room 109 typewriter
Typewriter paper
Pencils
Room 109 phonograph
Phonograph records
Room 109 electric heater
Map
Book
109 bottle of liquor
109 glasses
Hotel bell
Large poster
Room 110 telephone
Bottles of whiskey
Drinking glasses
Bottles with water
Newspapers
Breakfast tray
Pot of coffee
Coffee cup & saucer
'non egg' breakfast food
Plates
Cutlery
Napkin
Items to be packed including
   clothes

Cans of milk, corned beef,
    sugar, salmon. Bottles of
    cologne, bars of soap
Seguridad Headquarters
    phone
Writing pad
Seguridad Headquarters bell
Pencil
Room 109 electric cooking
    ring
Stew pot
Ladle
Tin of kippers

Can opener
2 room keys
2 tins of corned beef
Observation post telephone
Map
2 Telemeters
Sheaf of typed orders
Flashlight
Cigarettes
Matches
Rope
Adhesive tape

SOUND CUES

Ambient noise from street
Phone static—Dorothy's room
Offstage—traffic in hallway
Shelling begins—crash,
  whistling rush
Glass shards—residual crash
Banjo twang/crash—another
  shell
Banjo twang/crash—Closer
  shell
Another close shell—even
  larger
Phonograph—Chopin
  Mazurka Opus 33, no.4
Another shell—destruction
  in the street
Ambulance passes—clanging
Morning—People cry *El Sol*!
  Libertad!
Outside traffic, horns, dist
  machine guns
Dorothy rings bell for maid
Telephone rings
Water splashes/tap from
  bathroom
Phonograph—Chopin *Ballade*
  Op. 47
Record stopped—crackle
Distant traffic horn
Record spinning—creaking

Record wound—plays *Ballade*
Gunshot
Seguridad ambience—busy,
  doors
Antonio rings for guard
Distant church bell
Night ambience—couples
Something bubbles on stove
Distant gunfire
Comrades shout, laugh—sing
  Bandera
Comrades singing *Comintern*
Comrades singing *Partizan*
Distant church bell—time
Distant machine gun fire
Incoming shell, cries of
  children, chaos
Shell—dog yelps, cries
Another shell—long swishing
  rush
Shell—beyond the hotel
Distant people crying
Night ambience—observation
  post
Midnight bombardment—
  sharp percussive
Pounding thuds begin
Incoming shell—lands close by
Incoming shell—screaming
  rush

THE FIFTH COLUMN

The Fifth Column

ACT ONE • SCENE ONE

It is seven-thirty in the evening. A corridor on the first floor of the Hotel Florida in Madrid. There is a large white paper hand-printed sign on the door of Room 109 which reads, "Working, Do Not Disturb." TWO GIRLS with TWO SOLDIERS in International Brigade uniform pass along the corridor. One of the GIRLS stops and looks at the sign.

FIRST SOLDIER. Come on. We haven't got all night.

GIRL. What does it say?

[*The OTHER COUPLE have gone on down the corridor*]

SOLDIER. What does it matter what it says?

GIRL. No, read it to me. Be nice to me. Read to me in English.

SOLDIER. So that's what I'd draw. A literary one. The hell with it. I won't read it to you.

GIRL. You're not nice.

SOLDIER. I'm not supposed to be nice.

[*He stands off and looks at her unsteadily*]

Do I look nice? Do you know where I've just come from?

GIRL. I don't care where you come from. You all come from some place dreadful and you all go back there. All I asked you was to read me the sign. Come on then, if you won't.

SOLDIER. I'll read it to you. "Working. Do Not Disturb."

[*The* GIRL *laughs, a dry high, hard laugh*]

GIRL. I'll get me a sign like that too.

CURTAIN

ACT ONE • SCENE TWO

Curtain rises at once on Scene II. Interior of Room 109. There is a bed with a night table by it, two cretonne-covered chairs, a tall armoire with mirror, and a typewriter on another table. Beside the typewriter is a portable victrola. There is an electric heater which is glowing brightly, and a tall handsome blonde GIRL *is sitting in one of the chairs reading with her back to the lamp which is on the table beside the phonograph. Behind her are two large windows with their curtains drawn. There is a map of Madrid on the wall, and a* MAN *about thirty-five, wearing a leather jacket, corduroy trousers, and very muddy boots, is standing looking at it. Without looking up from her book, the girl, whose name is* DOROTHY BRIDGES, *says in a very cultivated voice:*

DOROTHY. Darling, there's one thing you really could do, and that's clean your boots before you come in here.

[*The man, whose name is* ROBERT PRESTON, *goes on looking at the map*]

And darling, don't you put your finger on it. It makes smudges.

[PRESTON *continues to look at the map*]

Darling, have you seen Philip?

PRESTON. Philip who?

DOROTHY. Our Philip.

PRESTON. [*Still looking at the map*] Our Philip was in Chicote's with that Moor that bit Rodgers, when I came up the Gran Via.

DOROTHY. Was he doing anything awful?

PRESTON. [*Still looking at the map*] Not yet.

DOROTHY. He will though. He's so full of life and good spirits.

PRESTON. The spirits are getting awfully bad at Chicote's.

DOROTHY. You make such dull jokes, darling. I wish Philip would come. I'm bored, darling.

PRESTON. Don't be a bored Vassar bitch.

DOROTHY. Don't call me names, please. I don't feel up to it just now. And besides, I'm not typical Vassar. I didn't understand *anything* they taught me there.

PRESTON. Do you understand anything that's happening here?

DOROTHY. No, darling. I understand a little bit about University City, but not too much. The Casa del Campo is a complete puzzle to me. And Usera—and Carabanchel. They're dreadful.

PRESTON. God, I wonder sometimes why I love you.

DOROTHY. I wonder why I love you, too, darling. I don't think it's very sensible, really. It's just sort of a bad habit I've gotten into. And Philip's so much more amusing, and so much *livelier*.

PRESTON. He's much livelier, all right. You know what he was doing last night before they shut Chicote's? He had a cuspidor, and he was going around blessing people out of it. You know, sprinkling it on them. It was better than ten to one he'd get shot.

DOROTHY. But he never does. I wish he'd come.

PRESTON. He will. He'll be here as soon as Chicote's shuts.

[*There is a knock at the door*]

DOROTHY. It's Philip. Darling, it's Philip.

[*The door opens to admit the* MANAGER *of the hotel. He is a dark, plump little man, who collects stamps, and speaks extraordinary English*]

Oh, it's the Manager.

MANAGER. How're you, very well, Mr. Preston? How're you, all right, Miss? I just come by see you have any little thing of any kind of sort you don't want to eat. Everything all right, everybody absolutely comfortable?

DOROTHY. Everything's marvelous, now the heater's fixed.

MANAGER. With a heater always is continually trouble. Electricity is a science not yet dominated by the workers. Also, the electrician drinks himself into a stupidity.

PRESTON. He didn't seem awfully bright, the electrician.

MANAGER. Is bright. But the drink. Always the drink. Then rapidly the failing to concentrate on electricity.

PRESTON. Then why do you keep him on?

MANAGER. Is the electrician of the committee. Frankly resembles a catastrophe. Is now in 113 drinking with Mr. Philip.

DOROTHY. [*Happily*] Then Philip's home.

MANAGER. Is more than home.

PRESTON. What do you mean?

MANAGER. Difficult to say before lady.

DOROTHY. Ring him up, darling.

PRESTON. I will not.

DOROTHY. Then I will.

[*She unhooks the telephone from the wall and says*]

Ciento trece— Hello. Philip? No. Come and see *us*. Please. Yes. All right.

[*She hooks up the phone again*]

He's coming.

MANAGER. Highly preferable he does not come.

PRESTON. Is it that bad?

MANAGER. Is worse. Is an unbelievable.

DOROTHY. Philip's marvelous. He does go about with dreadful people though. Why does he, I wonder?

MANAGER. I come another time. Maybe perhaps if you receive too much of anything you unable to eat always very welcome in the house where family constantly hungry unable understand lack of food. Thank you to another time. Good-bye.

[*He goes out just before the arrival of* MR. PHILIP *nearly bumping into him in the hallway. Outside the door he is heard to say*]:

Good afternoon, Mr. Philip.

[*A deep voice says very jovially*]

PHILIP. Salud, Comrade Stamp Collector. Picked up any valuable new issues lately?

[*In a quiet voice*]

MANAGER. No, Mr. Philip. Is have people from very dull countries lately. Is a plague of five cent U. S. and three francs fifty French. Is needed comrades from New Zealand written to by airmail.

PHILIP. Oh, they'll come. We're just in a dull epoch now. The shellings upset the tourist season. Be plenty of delegations when it slacks off again.

[*In a low non-joking voice*]

What's on your mind?

MANAGER. Always a little something.

PHILIP. Don't worry, that's all set.

MANAGER. Am worry a little just the same.

PHILIP. Take it easy.

MANAGER. You be careful, Mr. Philip.

[*In to the door comes* MR. PHILIP, *very large, very hearty, and wearing rubber boots*]

Salud, Comrade Bastard Preston. Salud Comrade Boredom Bridges. How are you comrades doing? Let me present an electrical comrade. Come in, Comrade Marconi. Don't stand out there.

[*A very small and quite drunken electrician, wearing soiled blue overalls, espadrilles, and a blue beret, comes in the door*]

ELECTRICIAN. Salud, Camaradas.

DOROTHY. Well. Yes. Salud.

PHILIP. And here's a Moorish comrade. You could say *the* Moorish comrade. Almost unique a Moorish comrade. She's awfully shy. Come in, Anita.

[*Enter a* MOORISH TART *from Cueta. She is very dark, but well built, kinky-haired and tough looking, and not at all shy*]

MOORISH TART. [*Defensively*] Salud, Camaradas.

PHILIP. This is the comrade that bit Vernon Rodgers that time. Laid him up for three weeks. Hell of a bite.

DOROTHY. Philip, darling, you couldn't just muzzle the comrade while she's here, could you?

MOORISH TART. Am insult.

PHILIP. The Moorish comrade learned English in Gibraltar. Lovely place, Gibraltar. I had a most unusual experience there once.

PRESTON. Let's not hear about it.

PHILIP. You *are* gloomy, Preston. You haven't got the party line right on that. All that long-faced stuff is out, you know. We're practically in a period of jubilation now.

PRESTON. I wouldn't talk about things you know nothing about.

PHILIP. Well, I see nothing to be gloomy about. What about offering these comrades some sort of refreshment?

MOORISH TART. [*To* DOROTHY] You got nice place.

DOROTHY. So good of you to like it.

MOORISH TART. How you keep from be evacuate?

DOROTHY. Oh, I just stay on.

MOORISH TART. How you eat?

DOROTHY. Not always too well, but we bring in tinned things from Paris in the Embassy pouch.

MOORISH TART. You what, Embassy pouch?

DOROTHY. Tinned things, you know. *Civet lièvre. Foie gras.* We had some really delicious *Poulet de Bresse.* From Bureau's.

MOORISH TART. You make fun me?

DOROTHY. Oh, no. Of course not. I mean we eat those things.

MOORISH TART. I eat water soup.

[*She stares at* DOROTHY *belligerently*]

What's a matter? You no like way I look? You think you better than me?

DOROTHY. Of course not. I'm probably *much* worse. Preston will tell you I'm *infinitely* worse. But we don't have to be comparative, do we? I mean in war time and all that, and you know all working for the same cause.

MOORISH TART. I scratch you eyes out if you think that.

DOROTHY. [*Appealingly, but very languid*] Philip, *please* talk to your friends and make them happy.

PHILIP. Anita, listen to me.

MOORISH TART. O.K.

PHILIP. Anita. Dorothy here is a lovely woman——

MOORISH TART. No lovely woman this business.

ELECTRICIAN. [*Standing up*] *Camaradas me voy.*

DOROTHY. What does he say?

PRESTON. He says he's going.

PHILIP. Don't believe him. He always says that.

[*To* ELECTRICIAN]

Comrade, you must stay.

ELECTRICIAN. *Camaradas entonces me quedo.*

DOROTHY. What?

PRESTON. He says he'll stay.

PHILIP. That's more like it, old man. You wouldn't rush off and leave us, would you, Marconi? No. An electrical comrade can be depended on to the last.

PRESTON. I thought it was a cobbler that stuck to the last.

DOROTHY. Darling, if you make jokes like that I'll leave you. I promise you.

MOORISH TART. Listen. All time talk. No time anything else. What we do here?

[*To* PHILIP]

You with me? Yes or no?

PHILIP. You put things so flatly, Anita.

MOORISH TART. Want a answer.

PHILIP. Well then, Anita, it must be in the negative.

MOORISH TART. What you mean? Take picture?

PRESTON. You see connection? Camera, take picture, negative? Charming, isn't it? She's so primitive.

MOORISH TART. What you mean take picture? You think me spy?

PHILIP. No, Anita. Please be reasonable. I just meant I wasn't with you any more. Not just now. I mean it's more or less off just for now.

MOORISH TART. No? You no with me?

PHILIP. No, my pretty one.

MOORISH TART. You with her?

[*Nodding toward* DOROTHY]

PHILIP. Possibly not.

DOROTHY. It *would* need a certain amount of discussion.

MOORISH TART. O.K. I scratch her eyes out.

[*She moves toward* DOROTHY]

ELECTRICIAN. *Camaradas, tengo que trabajar.*

DOROTHY. What does he say?

PRESTON. He says he must go to work.

PHILIP. Oh, don't pay attention to him. He gets these extraordinary ideas. It's an *idée fixe* he has.

ELECTRICIAN. *Camaradas, soy analfabético.*

PRESTON. He says he can't read or write.

PHILIP. Comrade, I mean, I mean, but really, you know, if we hadn't all gone to school we'd be in the same fix. Don't give it a thought, old man.

MOORISH TART. [*To* DOROTHY] O.K. I suppose, yes, all right. Downa hatch. Cheerio. Chin chin. Yes, O.K. Only one thing.

DOROTHY. But what, Anita.

MOORISH TART. You gotta take sign down.

DOROTHY. What sign?

MOORISH TART. Sign outside door. All the time working, isn't fair.

DOROTHY. And I've had a sign like that on my room door ever since college and it's never meant a thing.

MOORISH TART. You take down?

PHILIP. Of course she'll take it down. Won't you, Dorothy?

DOROTHY. Certainly, I'll take it down.

PRESTON. You never do work anyway.

DOROTHY. No, darling. But I always mean to. And I am going to finish that *Cosmopolitan* article just as soon as I understand things the *least* bit better.

> [*There is a crash outside the window in the street, followed by an incoming whistling rush, and another crash. You hear pieces of brick and steel falling, and the tinkle of falling glass*]

PHILIP. They're shelling again.

> [*He says it very quietly and soberly*]

PRESTON. The bastards.

> [*He says it very bitterly and rather nervously*]

PHILIP. You'd best open your windows, Bridges, my girl. There aren't any more panes now and winter's coming, you know.

MOORISH TART. You take the sign down?

[DOROTHY *goes to the door and removes the sign, taking out the thumbtacks with a nail file. She hands it to* ANITA]

DOROTHY. You keep it. Here are the thumbtacks too.

[DOROTHY *goes to the electric light and switches it off. Then opens both the windows. There is a sound like a giant banjo twang and an incoming rush like an elevated train or a subway train coming toward you. Then a third great crash, this time followed by a shower of glass*]

MOORISH TART. You good comrade.
DOROTHY. No. I'm not, but I would like to be.
MOORISH TART. You O.K. with me.

[*They are standing side by side in the light that comes in from the open door into the corridor*]

PHILIP. Having them open saved them from the concussion that time. You can hear the shells leave the battery. Listen for the next one.
PRESTON. I hate these damned night shellings.
DOROTHY. How long did the last one go on?
PHILIP. Just over an hour.
MOORISH TART. Dorothy, you think we better go in cave?

[*There is another banjo twang—a moment of quiet and then a great incoming rush, this time much closer, and at the crashing burst, the room fills with smoke and brick dust*]

PRESTON. The hell with it. I'm going down below.
PHILIP. This room has an excellent angle, really. I mean it. I could show you from the street.
DOROTHY. I think I'll just stay here. It doesn't make any difference where you wait for it.
ELECTRICAN. *Camaradas, no hay luz!*

[*He says this in a loud and almost prophetic voice, suddenly standing up and opening his arms wide*]

PHILIP. He says there isn't any light. You know the old boy is getting to be rather terrific. Like an electrical Greek chorus. Or a Greek electrical chorus.

PRESTON. I'm going to get out of here.

DOROTHY. Then, darling, will you take Anita and the electrician with you?

PRESTON. Come on.

[*They go as the next shell comes. The next shell is really something*]

DOROTHY. [*As they stand listening to the clattering of the brick and glass after the burst*] Philip, is the angle really safe?

PHILIP. It's as good here as anywhere. Really. Safe's not quite the word; but safety's hardly a thing people go in for any more.

DOROTHY. I feel safe with you.

PHILIP. Try to check that. That's a terrible phrase.

DOROTHY. But I can't help it.

PHILIP. Try very hard. That's a good girl.

[*He goes to the phonograph and puts on the Chopin Mazurka in C Minor, Opus 33, No. 4. They are listening to the music in the light from the glow of the electric heater*]

PHILIP. It's very thin and very old fashioned, but it's very beautiful.

[*Then comes the heavy banjo whang of the guns firing from Garabitas Hill. It whishes in with a roar and bursts in the street outside the window, making a bright flash through the window*]

DOROTHY. Oh darling, darling, darling.

PHILIP. [*Holding her*] Couldn't you use some other term? I've heard you call so many people that.

[*You hear the clanging of an ambulance. Then in the quiet the phonograph goes on playing the Mazurka as the——*]

CURTAIN COMES DOWN

ACT ONE · SCENE THREE

Rooms 109 and 110 in the Hotel Florida. The windows are open and sunlight is pouring in. There is an open door between them and over this door has been tacked, to the framework of the door, a large war poster so that when the door opens the open doorway is blocked by this poster. Still the door can open. It is open now, and the poster is like a large paper screen between the two rooms. There is a space perhaps two feet high between the bottom of the poster and the floor. In the bed in 109 DOROTHY BRIDGES *is asleep. In the bed in 110* PHILIP RAWLINGS *is sitting up looking out of the window. Through the window comes the sound of a man crying the daily papers. "El Sol! Libertad! El A.B.C. de Hoy!" There is a sound of a motor horn passing and then the distant clatter of machine-gun fire.* PHILIP *reaches for the telephone.*

PHILIP. Send up the morning papers, please. Yes. All of them.

[*He looks around the room and then out of the window. He looks at the war poster which shows transparent across the doorway in the bright morning sunlight.*]

No.

[*Shakes his head*]

Don't like it. Too early in the morning.

[*There is a knock at the door*]

Adelante.

[*There is another knock*]

Come in. Come in!

[*The door opens. It is the* MANAGER *holding the papers in his hands*]

MANAGER. Good morning, Mr. Philip. Thank you very much. Good morning to you all right. Terrible things last night, eh?

PHILIP. Terrible things every night. Frightful.

[*He grins*]

Let's see the papers.

MANAGER. They tell me the bad news from the Asturias. Is almost finish there.

PHILIP. [*Looking at the papers*] Not in here though.

MANAGER. No, but I know *you* know.

PHILIP. Quite. I say, when did I get this room?

MANAGER. You don't remember, Mr. Philip? You don't remember last night?

PHILIP. No. Can't say I do. Mention something and see if I recall it.

MANAGER. [*In really horrified tones*] You don't remember, really?

PHILIP. [*Cheerily*] Not a thing. Little bombardment early in the evening. Chicote's. Yes. Brought Anita around for a little spot of good clean fun. No difficulty with her, I hope?

MANAGER. [*Shaking his head*] No. No. Not with Anita. Mr. Philip, you don't remember about Mr. Preston?

PHILIP. No. What was the gloomy beggar up to? Not suicide, I hope.

MANAGER. You unremember throw him out in street?

PHILIP. From here?

[*He looks from the bed out toward the window*]

Any sign of him below?

MANAGER. No, from entry when you coming in from Ministerio very late last night after go for communiqué.

PHILIP. Hurt him?

MANAGER. Stitches. Some stitches.

PHILIP. Why didn't you stop it? Why do you permit that sort of thing in a decent hotel?

MANAGER. Then you take his room.

[*Sadly and reprovingly*]

Mr. Philip. Mr. Philip.

PHILIP. [*Very cheerily, but slightly baffled*] It's a lovely day though, isn't it?

MANAGER. Oh yes, is a superbly day. A day for picnics in the country.

PHILIP. And what did Preston do? He's very well set up, you know. And so gloomy. Must have put up quite a struggle.

MANAGER. He in other room now.

PHILIP. Where?

MANAGER. One thirteen. Your old room.

PHILIP. And I'm here?

MANAGER. Yes, Mr. Philip.

PHILIP. And what's that horrible thing?

[*Looking at the transparent poster between the doors*]

MANAGER. Is a patriotic poster very beautiful. Has fine sentiment, only see backwards from here.

PHILIP. And what's it cover? Where's that lead to?

MANAGER. To lady's room, Mr. Philip. Now you have a suite of rooms just newly married happy couple I come see everything all right you need anything at all anyway ring and ask for me. Congratulations, Mr. Philip. More than congratulations absolutely.

PHILIP. Does the door bolt on this side?

MANAGER. Absolutely, Mr. Philip.

PHILIP. Then bolt it and get out and have them bring me some coffee.

MANAGER. Yes, sir, Mr. Philip. Don't be cross on beautiful day like this.

[*Then hurriedly*]

Please, Mr. Philip, also remember food situation Madrid; if by any chance too much food any kind including anything any little can any sort always at home demanding lack every sort. In a family now is seven peoples including, Mr. Philip you would not believe what I permit myself the luxury of, a mother-in-law. Everything she eats. Everything agrees with *her*. Also one son seventeen formerly a champion of natation. What you call it the breast stroke. Built like this——

[*He gestures to show an enormous chest and arms*]

Is eat? Mr. Philip you *cannot* believe. Is a champion also of the eating. You should see. That is only two of the seven.

PHILIP. I'll see what I can get. Have to get it from my room. If any calls come have them ring me here.

MANAGER. Thank you, Mr. Philip. You have a heart big as the street. Is outside to see you two comrades.

PHILIP. Tell them to come in.

[*All this time* DOROTHY BRIDGES, *in the other room, is sleeping soundly. She did not awaken during the first of the conversation between* PHILIP *and the* MANAGER, *but only stirred a little in the bed. Now that the door is closed and bolted nothing can be heard between the two rooms*]

[*Enter* TWO COMRADES *in I.B. uniform*]

FIRST COMRADE. All right. He got away.

PHILIP. What do you mean he got away?

FIRST COMRADE. He's gone, that's all.

PHILIP. [*Very quickly*] How?

FIRST COMRADE. You tell me how.

PHILIP. Let's not have any of that.

[*Turning to the* SECOND COMRADE, *in a very dry voice*]

What about it?

SECOND COMRADE. He's gone.

PHILIP. And where were you?

SECOND COMRADE. Between the elevator and the stairs.

PHILIP. [*To* FIRST COMRADE] And you?

FIRST COMRADE. Outside the door all night.

PHILIP. And what time did you leave those posts?

FIRST COMRADE. Not at all.

PHILIP. Better think it over. You know what you're risking, don't you?

FIRST COMRADE. I am very sorry, but he's gone and that's all there is to it.

PHILIP. Oh no, it's not, my boy.

[*He takes down the telephone and calls a number*]

Noventa y siete zero zero zero. Yes. Antonio? Please. Yes. He's not there yet? No. Send over to pick up two men please in room one thirteen at the Hotel Florida. Yes. Please. Yes.

[*He hangs up the telephone*]

FIRST COMRADE. And all we ever did——

PHILIP. Take your time. You're going to need a very good story indeed.

FIRST COMRADE. There isn't any story except what I told you.

PHILIP. Take your time. Don't be rushed. Just sit down and think it over. Remember you had him here in this hotel. Where he couldn't get past you.

[*He reads in the papers. The* TWO COMRADES *stand there glumly*]
[*Without looking at them*]

Sit down. Make yourselves comfortable.

SECOND COMRADE. Comrade, we——

PHILIP. [*Without looking at him*] Don't use that word.

[*The* TWO COMRADES *look at each other*]

FIRST COMRADE. Comrade——

PHILIP. [*Discarding a paper and taking up another*] I told you not to use that word. It doesn't sound good in your mouth.

FIRST COMRADE. Comrade Commissar, we want to say——

PHILIP. Save it.

FIRST COMRADE. Comrade Commissar, you must listen to me.

PHILIP. I'll listen to you later. Don't you worry, my lad. I listen to you. When you came in here you sounded snotty enough.

FIRST COMRADE. Comrade Commissar, please listen to me. I want to tell you.

PHILIP. You let a man get away that I wanted. You let a man get away that I needed. You let a man get away who is going to kill.

FIRST COMRADE. Comrade Commissar, please——

PHILIP. Please, that's a funny word to hear in a soldier's mouth.

FIRST COMRADE. I am not a soldier by profession.

PHILIP. When you put the uniform on you're a soldier.

FIRST COMRADE. I came to fight for an ideal.

PHILIP. That's awfully pretty. Now let me tell you something. You come to fight for an ideal say, and you get scared in an attack. You don't like the noise or something, and people get killed—and you don't like the look of it—and you get afraid to die—and you shoot yourself in the hand or foot to get the hell out of it because you can't stand it. Well you get shot for that and your ideal isn't going to save you, brother.

FIRST COMRADE. But I fought well. I wasn't any self-inflicted wound.

PHILIP. I never said you were. I was just trying to explain something to you. But I don't seem to make myself clear. I'm thinking, you see, what the man is going to do that you let get away, and how I'm going to get him in a nice fine place like that again before he kills somebody. You see I needed him very much and very much alive. And you let him go.

FIRST COMRADE. Comrade Commissar, if you do not believe me——

PHILIP. No, I don't believe you and I'm not a Commissar. I'm a policeman. I don't believe anything I hear and very little of what I see. What do you mean, believe you? Listen. You're out of luck. I have to try to find out if you did it on purpose. I don't look forward to that.

[*He pours himself a drink*]

And if you're smart you won't look forward to it either. And if you didn't do it on purpose the effect is just the same. There's only one thing about duty. You have to do it. And there's only one thing about orders. THEY ARE TO BE OBEYED. I could, given enough time, explain to you that discipline is kindness, but then, I don't explain things very well.

FIRST COMRADE. Please, Comrade Commissar——

PHILIP. Use that word once more and you'll irritate me.

FIRST COMRADE. Comrade Commissar.

PHILIP. Shut up. I haven't any manners—see? I have to use them so much I get tired of them. And they bore me. I have to talk to you in front of my boss. And cut out the Commissar part. I'm a cop. What you tell me now doesn't mean anything. You see it's my ass too, you know. If you didn't do it on purpose I wouldn't worry too much. I just have to know, you see. I tell you what. If you didn't do it on purpose I'll split it with you.

[*There is a knock at the door*]

Adelante.

[*The door opens and shows two* ASSAULT GUARDS *in blue uniforms, flat caps, with rifles*]

FIRST GUARD. *A sus órdenes mi comandante.*

PHILIP. Take these two men over to Seguridad. I'll be by later to talk to them.

FIRST GUARD. *A sus órdenes.*

[*The* SECOND COMRADE *starts for the door. The* ASSAULT GUARD *runs his hands up and down his flanks to see if he is armed*]

PHILIP. They're both armed. Disarm them and take them along.

[*To the* TWO COMRADES]

Good luck.

[*He says this sarcastically*]

Hope you come out fine.

[*The four go out, and you hear them going down in the hall. In the other room,* DOROTHY BRIDGES *stirs in bed, wakes, yawns, and stretching, reaches up for the bell that hangs by the bed. You hear the bell ring.* PHILIP *hears it ring too. There is a knock on his door*]

PHILIP. *Adelante.*

[*It is the* MANAGER, *very upset*]

MANAGER. Is arrest two Comrades.

PHILIP. Very bad Comrades. One anyway. Other may be perfectly all right.

MANAGER. Mr. Philip is too much happening near you right now. I tell you as friend. Try and keep a things quieter. Is no good come with so much happen all the time.

PHILIP. No. I guess not. And it's a pretty day too, isn't it? Or isn't it?

MANAGER. I tell you what you should do. You should make a day like this excursion and picnic in the country.

[*In the next room* DOROTHY BRIDGES *has put on dressing gown and slippers. She disappears into the bathroom, and when she comes out she is brushing her hair. Her hair*

*is very beautiful and she sits on the bed, in front of the
electric heater, brushing it. With no make-up on she looks
very young. She rings the bell again, and a* MAID *opens the
door. She is a little old woman of about sixty in a blue
blouse and apron*]

MAID. [PETRA] *Se puede?*

DOROTHY. Good morning, Petra.

PETRA. *Buenos dias, Señorita.*

[DOROTHY *gets into bed and* PETRA *puts the breakfast
tray down on the bed*]

DOROTHY. Petra, aren't there any eggs?

PETRA. No, Señorita.

DOROTHY. Is your mother better, Petra?

PETRA. No, Señorita.

DOROTHY. Have you had any breakfast, Petra?

PETRA. No, Señorita.

DOROTHY. Get a cup and have some of this coffee right away.
Hurry.

PETRA. I'll take some when you're through, Señorita. Was the
bombardment very bad here last night?

DOROTHY. Oh, it was *lovely.*

PETRA. Señorita, you say such dreadful things.

DOROTHY. No, but Petra it *was* lovely.

PETRA. In Progresso, in my quarter, there were six killed in one
floor. This morning they were taking them out and all the glass
gone in the street. There won't be any more glass this winter.

DOROTHY. Here there wasn't *any one* killed.

PETRA. Is the Señor ready for his breakfast?

DOROTHY. The Señor isn't here any more.

PETRA. He has gone to the front?

DOROTHY. Oh, no. He never goes to the front. He just writes
about it. There's *another* Señor here.

PETRA. [*Sadly*] Who, Señorita?

DOROTHY. [*Happily*] Mr. Philip.

PETRA. Oh, Señorita. How *terrible*.

[*She goes out crying*]

DOROTHY. [*Calling after her*] Petra. Oh, Petra!
PETRA. [*Resignedly*] Yes, Señorita.
DOROTHY. [*Happily*] See if Mr. Philip's up.
PETRA. Yes, Señorita.

[PETRA *comes to* MR. PHILIP'S *door and knocks*]

PHILIP. Come in.
PETRA. The Señorita asks me to see if you are up.
PHILIP. No.
PETRA. [*At the other door*] The Señor says he's not up.
DOROTHY. Tell him to come and have some breakfast, Petra, please.
PETRA. [*At the other door*] The Señorita asks you to come and have some breakfast, but there is very little as there is.
PHILIP. Tell the Señorita that I never eat breakfast.
PETRA. [*At the other door*] He says he never eats breakfast. But I know he eats more breakfast than three people.
DOROTHY. Petra, he's *so* difficult. Just ask him not to be stupid and come in here please.
PETRA. [*At the other door*] She says come.
PHILIP. What a word. What a word.

[*He puts on a dressing gown and slippers*]

These are rather small. Must be Preston's. Nice robe though. Might offer to buy it from him.

[*He gathers up the papers, opens the door and goes into the other room, knocking as he pushes the door open*]

DOROTHY. Come in. Oh, here you are.
PHILIP. Isn't this all very rather unconventional?
DOROTHY. Philip, you stupid darling. Where have you been?
PHILIP. In a very strange room.
DOROTHY. How did you get there?

PHILIP. No idea.

DOROTHY. Don't you remember *anything?*

PHILIP. I recall some muck about chucking someone out.

DOROTHY. That was *Preston.*

PHILIP. Really?

DOROTHY. Yes *very* really.

PHILIP. We must get him back. Shouldn't be rude that way.

DOROTHY. Oh, no. Philip. No. He's gone for good.

PHILIP. Awful phrase; for good.

DOROTHY. [*Determinedly*] For good and all.

PHILIP. Even worse phrase. Gives me the horrorous.

DOROTHY. What are the horrorous, darling?

PHILIP. Sort of super horrors. You know. Now you see them. Now you don't. Watch for them to go around the corner.

DOROTHY. You haven't had them?

PHILIP. Oh, yes. I've had everything. Worst I remember was a file of marines. Used to come into the room suddenly.

DOROTHY. Philip, sit here.

[PHILIP *sit downs on the bed very gingerly*]

Philip, you must promise me something. You won't just go on drinking and not have any aim in life and not do anything real? You aren't just going to be a Madrid playboy are you?

PHILIP. A *Madrid* playboy?

DOROTHY. Yes. Around Chicote's. And the Miami. And the embassies and the Ministerio and Vernon Rodgers' flat and that dreadful Anita. Though the embassies are really the worst. Philip, you *aren't,* are you?

PHILIP. What else is there?

DOROTHY. There's everything. You could do something serious and decent. You could do something brave and calm and good. You know what will happen if you keep on just crawling around from bar to bar and going with those dreadful people? You'll be shot. A man was shot the other night in Chicote's. It was terrible.

PHILIP. Any one we know?

DOROTHY. No. Just a poor man who was squirting every one

with a flit gun. He didn't mean any harm. And some one took offense and shot him. I saw it and it was *very* depressing. They shot him very suddenly and he lay on his back and his face was very gray and he'd been so gay just a little while before. They kept every one there for two hours, and the police smelt of everybody's pistol and they wouldn't serve any more drinks. They didn't cover him up and we had to go and show our papers to a man at a table just beside where he was and it was *very* depressing, Philip. And he had such dirty hose and his shoes were completely worn through on the bottoms and he had *no* undershirt at *all*.

PHILIP. Poor chap. You know the stuff they drink is absolutely poison now. Makes people quite mad.

DOROTHY. But Philip, *you* don't have to be like that. And *you* don't have to go around and maybe have people *shoot* at you. You could do something *political* or something *military* and fine.

PHILIP. Don't tempt me. Don't make me ambitious.

[*He pauses*]

Don't open vistas.

DOROTHY. That was a dreadful thing you did the other night with the spittoon. Trying to provoke trouble there in Chicote's. Simply trying to *provoke* it, everybody said.

PHILIP. And who was I provoking?

DOROTHY. I don't know. What does it matter who? You shouldn't be provoking *anybody*.

PHILIP. No, I suppose not. It probably comes soon enough without provoking it.

DOROTHY. Don't talk pessimistically, darling, when we've just started our life together.

PHILIP. Our——?

DOROTHY. Our life together. Philip, don't you want to have a long, happy, quiet life at some place like Saint-Tropez or, you know, some place like Saint-Tropez *was* and have long walks, and go swimming and have children and be happy and everything? I mean really. Don't you want all this to end? I mean you know, war and revolution?

PHILIP. And will we have the *Continental Daily Mail* for breakfast and *brioches* and fresh strawberry jam?

DOROTHY. Darling, we'll have *œufs au jambon* and you can have the *Morning Post* if you like. And every one will say Messieur-Dame.

PHILIP. The *Morning Post*'s just stopped publishing.

DOROTHY. Oh, Philip, you're so depressing. I wanted us to have *such* a happy life. Don't you want children? They can play in the Luxembourg and roll hoops and sail boats.

PHILIP. And you can show them on a map. You know; on a globe even. "Children"; we'll call the boy Derek, worst name I know. You can say, "Derek. That's the Wangpoo. Now follow my finger and I'll show you where Daddy is." And Derek will say, "Yes, Mummy. Have I ever seen Daddy?"

DOROTHY. Oh, no. It won't be like that. We'll just live somewhere where it's lovely and you'll write.

PHILIP. What?

DOROTHY. Whatever you like. Novels and articles and a book on this war perhaps.

PHILIP. Be a pretty book. Might make it with—with—you know—illustrations.

DOROTHY. Or you could study and write a book on politics. Books on politics sell *forever,* some one told me.

PHILIP. [*Ringing the bell*] I imagine.

DOROTHY. You could study and write a book on dialectics. There's *always* a market for a new book on dialectics.

PHILIP. Really?

DOROTHY. But, darling Philip, the first thing is for you to start here now and do something worth doing and stop this absolutely *utter* playboy business.

PHILIP. I read it in a book, but I never really knew about it. Is it true that the first thing an American woman does is try to get the man she's interested in to give up something? You know, boozing about, or smoking Virginia cigarettes, or wearing gaiters, or hunting, or something silly?

DOROTHY. No, Philip. It's that you're a very serious problem for any woman.

PHILIP. I hope so.

DOROTHY. And I don't want you to give up something. I want you to *take* up something.

PHILIP. Good.

[*He kisses her*]

I will. Now have some breakfast. I have to go back and make a few phone calls.

DOROTHY. Philip, don't go.

PHILIP. I'll be back in just a moment, darling. And I'll be *so* serious.

DOROTHY. You know what you said?

PHILIP. Of course.

DOROTHY. [*Very happily*] You said *Darling*.

PHILIP. I knew it was infectious but I never knew it was contagious. Forgive me, *dear*.

DOROTHY. *Dear* is a nice word, too.

PHILIP. Good-bye then—er—sweet.

DOROTHY. Sweet, oh you *darling*.

PHILIP. Good-bye, Comrade.

DOROTHY. Comrade. Oh, and you said darling before.

PHILIP. Comrade's quite a word. I suppose I oughtn't to chuck it around. I take it back.

DOROTHY. [*Rapturously*] Oh, Philip. *You're developing politically.*

PHILIP. God—er, oh you know, whatever it is, save us.

DOROTHY. Don't blaspheme. It's frightfully bad luck.

PHILIP. [*Hurriedly and rather grimly*] Good-bye, *darling dear sweet.*

DOROTHY. You don't call me *comrade*.

PHILIP. [*Going out*] No. You see I'm developing politically.

[*He goes into the next room*]

DOROTHY. [*Rings for* PETRA. *Speaks to her. Leaning back comfortably in bed against the pillows*] Oh, Petra, he's so lovely and so sort of *vital* and so gay. But he doesn't *do* anything. He's supposed to send dispatches to some stupid London paper, but they say at Censura he practically never sends anything. He's so *refreshing* after Preston always going on about his wife and children. Let him go *back* to his wife and children now if he's so excited about them. I'll bet he won't. Those wife-and-children men at a war. They just use them as sort of an opening wedge to get into bed with some one and then immediately afterwards they club you with them. I mean positively *club* you. I don't know why I ever put up with Preston so long. And he's *so* gloomy. Expecting the city to fall and everything and always looking at the map. Always looking at a map is one of the most irritating habits a man can get into. Isn't it, Petra?

PETRA. I don't understand, Señorita.

DOROTHY. Oh, Petra, I wonder what he's doing now.

PETRA. Nothing good.

DOROTHY. Petra, don't talk that way. You're a *defeatist*.

PETRA. No, Señorita, I have no politics. I only work.

DOROTHY. Well, you can go now because I think I'll go back to sleep for just a little while longer. I feel so sleepy and good this morning.

PETRA. That you rest well, Señorita.

[*She goes out closing the door*]
[*In the next room* PHILIP *answers the phone*]

PHILIP. Yes. Right. Send him up.

[*There is a knock on the door and a* COMRADE *in I.B. uniform enters. He salutes smartly. He is a young, good-looking, dark boy of perhaps twenty-three*]

Salud, Comrade. Come in.

COMRADE. They sent me here from Brigade. I was to report to you in room one thirteen.

PHILIP. The room's changed. Do you have a copy of the order?
COMRADE. It was a verbal order.

[PHILIP *takes the phone; asks for a number*]

PHILIP. *Ochenta—dos zero uno cinco.* Hello Haddock? No.
Haddock. Hake speaking. Yes, Hake. Good. Haddock?

[*He turns to the* COMRADE]

What's your name, Comrade?
COMRADE. Wilkinson.
PHILIP. Hello, Haddock. Sent a Comrade Wilkinson over to
the Booth Fisheries? Right. Thanks so much. Salud.

[*Hooks up the telephone. He turns to the* COMRADE *and
puts out his hand*]

I'm glad to see you, Comrade. Now what was it?
COMRADE. I'm under your orders.
PHILIP. Oh.

[*He seems very reluctant, about something*]

How old are you, Comrade?
COMRADE. Twenty.
PHILIP. Had much fun?
COMRADE. I'm not in this for fun.
PHILIP. No. Of course not. Was just a question.

[*He pauses. Then goes on abandoning the reluctance; he
speaks in a very military way*]

Now one thing I have to tell you. In this particular show you have
to be armed to enforce your authority. But you're not to use your
weapon under any circumstances. Under any circumstances. Is that
quite clear?
COMRADE. Not in self-defense?
PHILIP. Not under *any circumstances*.
COMRADE. I see. And what are my orders?

PHILIP. Go down and take yourself a walk. Then come back here and take a room and register. When you have the room stop by here and let me know what room it is, and I'll tell you what to do. You'll have to spend most of your time in your room today.

[*He pauses*]

Have a good walk. Might have a glass of beer. There's beer today at the Aguilar places.

COMRADE WILKINSON. I don't drink, Comrade.

PHILIP. Quite right. Excellent. We of the older generation have certain leprous spots of vice which can hardly be eradicated at this date. But you are an example to us. Get along now.

COMRADE WILKINSON. Yes, Comrade.

[*He salutes and goes out*]

PHILIP. [*After he has gone*] Awful pity. Yes. An awful pity.

[*The telephone rings*]

Yes? Here speaking. Good. No. I'm sorry. Later.

[*He hangs up the phone. . . . The phone rings again*]

Oh, hello. Yes. I'm awfully sorry. What a shame. I will. Yes. Later.

[*He hangs up. The phone rings again*]

Oh, hello. Oh, I am sorry, I really am. What do you say to a little later? No? Good man. Come in and we'll get it over with.

[*There is a knock at the door*]

Come on in.

[*Enter* PRESTON. *He has a bandaged eyebrow and looks none too well*]

I *am* sorry, you know.

PRESTON. What good does that do? You behaved disgustingly.

PHILIP. Right. Now what can I do?

[*Spoken very flatly*]

I said I was sorry.

PRESTON. Well, you might take off my dressing gown and slippers.

PHILIP. [*Taking them off*] Good.

[*He hands them over*]
[*Regretfully*]

You wouldn't sell the robe, would you? It's nice stuff.

PRESTON. No. And now get out of my room.

PHILIP. Do we have to do the whole thing over again?

PRESTON. If you won't get out I'll ring and have you thrown out.

PHILIP. Better ring, then.

[PRESTON *rings.* PHILIP *goes into the bathroom. There is a sound of water splashing. There is a knock at the door and the* MANAGER *enters*]

MANAGER. Nothing is all right?

PRESTON. I want you to call the police and have this man removed from my room.

MANAGER. Mr. Preston. I have maid pack your things up right away. You be comfortable in one fourteen. Mr. Preston you know better than call police into a hotel. What's a first thing police say? Whosa cana milk belong to? Whosa corn beef belong to? Whosa hoards coffee in this hotel? Whatsa meaning all this sugar in the armoire? Whosa got three bottles of whiskey? Whatsa matter here? Mr. Preston never calla police in private matter. Mr. Preston, I appeal to you.

PHILIP. [*From the bathroom*] Whosa these three cakesa soap belong to?

MANAGER. You see, Mr. Preston? In a private matter public authority is giva always a wrong interpretation. Is a law against to have these things. Is a severe law against all forms of hoarding. Is a police misunderstand.

PHILIP. [*From the bathroom*] Whosa got three bottles eau de cologne in here?

MANAGER. You see, Mr. Preston? With all my good voluntaries I could not introduce police.

PRESTON. Oh, go to—hell then, both of you. Have the things moved into one fourteen then. You're a rotten cad, Rawlings. Remember I told you, will you?

PHILIP. [*From the bathroom*] Whosa four tubes Mennen's shaving cream belong to?

MANAGER. Mister Preston. *Four* tubes. Mister Press-ton.

PRESTON. All you do is beg for food. I've given you plenty. Pack up the things and have them moved.

MANAGER. Very good, Mister Preston, but only one thing. When against all my voluntaries initiate slight petition for food only wishing superating quantities——

PHILIP. [*From bathroom, choking with laughing*] What's that?

MANAGER. Am telling Mr. Preston only petition unnecessary amounts and then only on basis of seven in family. Listen, Mr. Preston, has my mother-in-law—that luxury—now in her head one tooth remaining. You understand. Only one tooth. With this eats all and enjoys. When this goes must I buy entire apparatus of teeth both higher and lower, and is fit for eating higher things. Is fit for the *beef*steak, is fit for the chops, is fit for the what you call it, the *salomillo*. Every night I tell you, Mr. Preston, I ask her how is the tooth old woman? Every night I think if that goes where are *we*? Given entire new up and down teeth would not be enough horses left in Madrid for the army. I tell you, Mr. Preston, you never saw such a woman. Such a luxury. Mr. Preston, you unable spare one small can of any sort that superates?

PRESTON. Get something from Rawlings. He's your friend.

PHILIP. [*Coming out of the bathroom*] With me Comrade Stamp Collector superates one can of bully beef.

MANAGER. Oh, Mr. Philip. You have heart bigger than the hotel.

PRESTON. And twice as dirty.

[*He goes out*]

PHILIP. He's very bitter.

MANAGER. You take away the young lady. Makes him *furious*. Fills him with, how you call, jellishness.

PHILIP. That's it. He's simply crammed with jellishness. Tried to knock some of it out of him last night. No good.

MANAGER. Listen, Mr. Philip. Tell me one thing. How long the war going last?

PHILIP. A long time, I'm afraid.

MANAGER. Mr. Philip, I hate to hear you say *so*. Is now a year. Is not funny, you know.

PHILIP. Don't you worry about it. You just last yourself.

MANAGER. You be careful and last too. Mr. Philip, be more careful. I know. Don't think I don't know.

PHILIP. Don't know too much. And whatever you know keep your good old mouth shut, eh? We work all right together that way.

MANAGER. But be careful, Mr. Philip.

PHILIP. I'm lasting all right. Have a drink?

[*He pours a Scotch and puts water in it*]

MANAGER. Never I touch the alcohol. But listen, Mr. Philip. Be more careful. In one o five is very bad. In one o seven is very bad.

PHILIP. Thanks. I know that. Only what I had in one o seven I lost. They let him get away.

MANAGER. In one fourteen is only a fool.

PHILIP. Quite.

MANAGER. Last night is try get into one thirteen for you, pretending was mistake. I know.

PHILIP. That's why I wasn't there. I had some one looking after the fool.

MANAGER. Mr. Philip, you be very careful. You like I should put the Yale lock on door? The big lock? Very strongest type?

PHILIP. No. The big lock wouldn't do any good. You don't do this business with big locks.

MANAGER. You want anything special, Mr. Philip? Anything can do?

PHILIP. No. Nothing special. Thanks for turning away that fool journalist from Valencia who wanted a room here. We've got enough fools here now including you and me.

MANAGER. But I let him in later if you want. I told him was no room would let him know. If things quiet can let him in later on. Mr. Philip, you take care yourself. Please. You know.

PHILIP. I'm lasting well enough. I just get sort of low in my mind sometimes.

[*During this time* DOROTHY BRIDGES *has gotten out of bed, gone into the bathroom, dressed and come back to the room. She sits at the typewriter, then gets up and puts a record on the gramophone. It is a Chopin Ballade in La Bemol Menor Op. 47.* PHILIP *hears the music*]

PHILIP. [*To the* MANAGER] Excuse me a moment, will you? You going to move his things? If any one comes in for me ask them to wait, will you?

MANAGER. I tell the maid that moves.

[PHILIP *goes to* DOROTHY'S *door and knocks*]

DOROTHY. Come in, Philip.

PHILIP. Mind if I have a drink in here for a moment?

DOROTHY. No. Please do.

PHILIP. Two things I'd like to ask you to do.

[*The record has stopped. In the other room you see that the* MANAGER *has gone out and that the* MAID *has come in and is making a pile of* PRESTON'S *things on the bed*]

DOROTHY. What are they, Philip?

PHILIP. One is move out of this hotel, and the other is go back to America.

DOROTHY. Why, you impudent, impertinent man. Why you're worse than Preston.

PHILIP. I mean them both. This hotel's no place for you now. I mean it.

DOROTHY. And I was just beginning to be so happy with you. Philip, don't be silly. Please, darling, don't be silly.

[*At the door of the other room you see the* YOUNG COMRADE WILKINSON *in I.B. uniform at the open door*]

WILKINSON. [*To the* MAID] Comrade Rawlings?

MAID. Come in and sit down. He said to wait.

[WILKINSON *sits down in a chair with his back to the door. In the other room* DOROTHY *has put the record on the phonograph again.* PHILIP *lifts the needle off, and the record goes round and round on the turntable*]

DOROTHY. You said you wanted a drink. Here.

PHILIP. I don't want one.

DOROTHY. What's the matter, darling?

PHILIP. You know I'm being serious. You must get out of here.

DOROTHY. I'm not afraid of the shelling. You know that.

PHILIP. It's not the shelling.

DOROTHY. Well then, what is it, darling? Don't you like me? I'd like to make you very happy here.

PHILIP. What can I do to make you get out?

DOROTHY. Nothing. I won't go.

PHILIP. I'll have you moved over to the Victoria.

DOROTHY. You *will* not.

PHILIP. I wish I could talk to you.

DOROTHY. But why can't you?

PHILIP. I can't ever talk to any one.

DOROTHY. But darling, that's just an inhibition. You could go to an analyst and have that fixed in no time. It's easy and it's very fascinating.

PHILIP. You're hopeless. But you're beautiful. I'll just have you moved out.

[*He puts the needle back on the record and winds up the phonograph*]

PHILIP. I'm sorry if I seem dismal.

DOROTHY. It's probably just your liver, darling.

[*As the record plays, you see that some one has stopped outside the door of the room where the* MAID *is working and the boy is sitting. The man is wearing a beret and a trench coat, and he leans against the door jamb to steady his aim and shoots the boy in the back of his head with a long-barrelled Mauser pistol. The* MAID *screams— "Ayee"— then starts to cry into her apron.* PHILIP, *as he hears the shot, pushes* DOROTHY *toward the bed and goes to the door with a pistol in his right hand. Opening the door he looks both ways from it keeping himself covered, then rounds the corner and enters the room. As the* MAID *sees him with the pistol she screams again*]

PHILIP. Don't be silly.

[*He goes over to the chair where the body is, lifts the head and lets it drop*]

The bastards. The dirty bastards.

[DOROTHY *had followed him to the door. He pushes her out*]

PHILIP. Get out of here.

DOROTHY. Philip, what is it?

PHILIP. Don't look at him. That's a dead man. Somebody shot him.

DOROTHY. Who shot him?

PHILIP. Maybe he shot himself. It's none of your business. Get out of here. Didn't you ever see a dead man before? Aren't you a lady war correspondent or something? Get out of here and go and write an article. This is none of your business.

[*Then to the* MAID]

Hurry up and get those cans and bottles out of here.

[*He commences to throw things from the armoire shelves onto the bed*]

All the cans of milk. *All* the corn beef. *All* the sugar. *All* the tinned salmon. *All* the eau de cologne. *All* the extra soap. Get them out. We have to call the police.

CURTAIN

END OF ACT I

ACT TWO • SCENE ONE

A room in Seguridad headquarters. There is a plain table, bare except for a green-shaded lamp. The windows are all closed and shuttered. Behind the table a short man with a very thin-lipped, hawk-nosed ascetic-looking face is sitting. He has very thick eyebrows. PHILIP *sits on a chair beside the table. The hawk-faced man is holding a pencil. On a chair in front of the table a* MAN *is sitting. He is crying with very deep shaking sobs.* ANTONIO (*the hawk-nosed man*) *is looking at him very interestedly. It is the* FIRST COMRADE *from Scene III, Act I. He is bareheaded, his tunic is off, and his braces, which hold up his baggy I.B. trousers, hang down along his trousers. As the curtain rises* PHILIP *stands up and looks at the* FIRST COMRADE.

PHILIP. [*In a tired voice*] I'd like to ask you one more thing.

FIRST COMRADE. Don't ask me. Please don't ask me. I don't want you to ask me.

PHILIP. Were you asleep?

FIRST COMRADE. [*Choking*] Yes.

PHILIP. [*In a very tired flat voice*] You know the penalty for that?

FIRST COMRADE. Yes.

PHILIP. Why didn't you say so at the start and save a lot of trouble? I wouldn't have you shot for that. I'm just disappointed in you now. Do you think people shoot people for fun?

FIRST COMRADE. I should have told you. I was frightened.

PHILIP. Yeah. You should have told me.

FIRST COMRADE. Truly, Comrade Commissar.

PHILIP. [*To* ANTONIO, *coldly*] You think he was asleep?

ANTONIO. How do I know? Do you want me to question him?

PHILIP. No, *mi Coronel*, no. We want information. We don't want a confession.

[*To the* FIRST COMRADE]

Listen, what did you dream about when you went to sleep?

FIRST COMRADE. [*Checks himself sobbing, hesitates, then goes on*] I don't remember.

PHILIP. Just try to. Take your time. I only want to be sure, you see. Don't try to lie. I'll know if you lie.

FIRST COMRADE. I remember now. I was against the wall and my rifle was between my legs when I leaned back, and I remember.

[*He chokes*]

In the dream I—I thought it was my girl and she was doing something—kind of funny—to me. I don't know what it was. It was just in a dream.

[*He chokes*]

PHILIP. [*To* ANTONIO] You satisfied now?

ANTONIO. I do not understand it completely.

PHILIP. Well, I guess nobody really understands it completely, but he's convinced me.

[*To the* FIRST COMRADE]

What's your girl's name?

FIRST COMRADE. Alma.

PHILIP. O.K. When you write her tell her she brought you a lot of luck.

[*To* ANTONIO]

As far as I'm concerned you can take him out. He reads the *Worker*. He knows Joe North. He's got a girl named Alma. He's got a good record with the Brigade, and he went to sleep and let a citizen slip who shot a boy named Wilkinson by mistake for me.

The thing to do is to give him lots of strong coffee to keep him awake and keep rifles out from between his legs. Listen, Comrade, I'm sorry if I spoke roughly to you in the performance of my duty.

ANTONIO. I would like to put a few questions.

PHILIP. Listen, *mi Coronel*. If I wasn't good at this you wouldn't have let me go on doing it so long. This boy is all right. You know we are none of us *exactly* what you would call all *right*. But this boy is pretty all right. He just went to sleep, and I'm not justice you know. I'm just working for you, and the cause, and the Republic and one thing and another. And we used to have a President named Lincoln in America, you know, who commuted sentences of sentries to be shot for sleeping, you know. So I think if it's all right with you we'll just sort of commute his sentence. He comes from the Lincoln Battalion you see—and it's an awfully good battalion. It's such a good battalion and it's done such things that it would break your damn heart if I tried to tell you about it. And if I was in it I'd feel decent and proud instead of the way I feel doing what I am. But I'm not, see? I'm a sort of a second-rate cop pretending to be a third-rate newspaperman—But listen Comrade Alma——

[*Turning to prisoner*]

If you ever go to sleep again on duty when you are working for me I'll shoot you myself, see? You *hear* me? And write it to Alma.

ANTONIO. [*Ringing. Two* ASSAULT GUARDS *come in*] Take him away. You speak very confusedly, Philip. But you have a certain amount of credit to exhaust.

FIRST COMRADE. Thank you, Comrade Commissar.

PHILIP. Oh, don't say thank you in a war. This is a war. You don't say thank you in it. But you're welcome, see? And when you write to Alma tell her she brought you a lot of luck.

[FIRST COMRADE *goes out with* ASSAULT GUARDS]

ANTONIO. Yes, and now. This man got away from room 107 and shot this boy by mistake for you, and who is this man?

PHILIP. Oh, I don't know. Santa Claus, I guess. He's got a number. They have A numbered one to ten, and B numbered one to ten, and C numbered one to ten, and they shoot people and they blow up things and they do everything you're overly familiar with. And they work very hard, and aren't really awfully efficient. But they kill a lot of people that they shouldn't kill. The trouble is they've worked it out so well on the lines of the old Cuban A.B.C. that unless you get somebody outside that they deal with, it doesn't mean anything. It's just like cutting the heads off boils instead of listening to a Fleischman's Yeast Program. You know, correct me if I become confusing.

ANTONIO. And why do you not take this man with a sufficient force?

PHILIP. Because I cannot afford to make much noise and scare others that we need much more. This one is just a killer.

ANTONIO. Yes. There are plenty of fascists left in a town of a million people, and they work inside. Those who have the courage to. We must have twenty thousand active here.

PHILIP. More. Double that. But when you catch them they won't talk. Except the politicians.

ANTONIO. Politicians. Yes, politicians. I have seen a politician on the floor in that corner of the room unable to stand up when it was time to go out. I have seen a politician walk across that floor on his knees and put his arms around my legs and kiss my feet. I watched him slobber on my boots when all he had to do was such a simple thing as die. I have seen many die, and I have never seen a politician die well.

PHILIP. I don't like to see them die. It's O.K. I guess, if you like to see it. But I don't like it. Sometimes I don't know how you stick it. Listen, who dies well?

ANTONIO. You know. Don't be naïve.

PHILIP. Yes. I suppose I know.

ANTONIO. I could die all right. I don't ask any one to do something that is impossible.

PHILIP. You're a specialist. Look, Tonico. Who dies well? Go ahead, say it. Go ahead. Do you good to talk about your trade. Talk about it you know. Then next thing you know, forget it. Simple, eh? Tell me about in the first days of the movement.

ANTONIO. [*Rather proudly*] You want to hear? You mean definite people?

PHILIP. No. I know a couple of definite people. I mean sort of by classes.

ANTONIO. Fascists, real fascists, the young ones; very well. Sometimes with very much style. They are mistaken, but they have much style. Soldiers, yes, the majority all right. Priests all my life I am against. The church fights us. We fight the church. I am a Socialist for many years. We are the oldest revolutionary party in Spain. But to die——

[*He shakes his hand in the quick triple flip of the wrist that is the Spanish gesture of supreme admiration*]

To die? Priests? Terrific. You know; just simple priests. I don't mean bishops.

PHILIP. And Antonio. Sometimes there must have been mistakes, eh? When you had to work in a hurry perhaps. Or you know, just mistakes, we all make mistakes. I just made a little one yesterday. Tell me, Antonio, were there ever any mistakes?

ANTONIO. Oh, yes. Certainly. Mistakes. Oh, yes. Mistakes. Yes. Yes. Very regrettable mistakes. A very few.

PHILIP. And how did the mistakes die?

ANTONIO. [*Proudly*] All very well.

PHILIP. Ah——

[*It is noise a boxer might make when he is hit with a hard body punch*]

And this trade we're in now. You know, what's the silly name they call it? Counter-espionage. It doesn't ever get on your nerves?

ANTONIO. [*Simply*] No.

PHILIP. With me it's on the nerves now for a long time.

ANTONIO. But you've only been doing it for a little while.

PHILIP. Twelve bloody months, my boy, in this country. And before that, Cuba. Ever been in Cuba?

ANTONIO. Yes.

PHILIP. That's where I got sucked in on all this.

ANTONIO. How were you sucked in?

PHILIP. Oh, people started trusting me that should have known better. And I suppose because they should have known better I started getting, you know, sort of trustworthy. You know, not elaborately, just sort of moderately trustworthy. And then they trust you a little more and you do it all right. And then you know, you get to believing in it. Finally I guess you get to liking it. I have a sort of a feeling I don't explain it very well.

ANTONIO. You're a good boy. You work well. Everybody trusts you very much.

PHILIP. Too bloody much. And I'm tired too, and I'm worried right now. You know what I'd like? I'd like to never kill another son-of-a-bitch, I don't care who or for what, as long as I live. I'd like to never have to lie. I'd like to know who I'm with when I wake up. I'd like to wake up in the same place every morning for a week straight. I'd like to marry a girl named Bridges that you don't know. But don't mind if I use the name because I like to say it. And I'd like to marry her because she's got the longest, smoothest, straightest legs in the world, and I don't have to listen to her when she talks if it doesn't make too good sense. But I'd like to see what the kids would look like.

ANTONIO. She is the tall blonde with that correspondent?

PHILIP. Don't talk about her like that. She isn't any tall blonde with some correspondent. That's my girl. And if I talk too much or take up your valuable time, why, stop me. You know I'm a very extraordinary fellow. I can talk either English or American. Was brought up in one, raised in the other. That's what I make my living at.

ANTONIO. [*Soothingly*] I know. You are tired, Philip.

PHILIP. Well, now I'm talking American. Bridges is the same way. Only I'm not sure she can talk American. You see she learned her English at college and from the cheap or literary type of Lord, but you know what's funny, you see. I just like to hear her talk. I don't care what she says. I'm relaxed now, you see. I haven't had anything to drink since breakfast, and I'm a lot drunker than I am when I drink, and that's a bad sign. Is it all right for one of your operatives to relax, *mi Coronel?*

ANTONIO. You ought to go to bed. You're tired out, Philip, and you have much work to do.

PHILIP. That's right. I'm tired out and I have much work to do. I'm waiting to meet a comrade at Chicote's. Name of Max. I have, and I do not exaggerate, very much work to do. Max, whom I believe you know and who, to show what a distinguished man he is, has no hind name, while my back name is Rawlings exactly the same as when I started. Which shows you I haven't gotten *very* far in this business. What was I saying?

ANTONIO. About Max.

PHILIP. Max. That's it. Max. Well he's a day overdue now. He's been navigating now for about two weeks, say circulating to avoid confusion, behind the fascist lines. It's his specialty. And he says, and he doesn't lie. I lie. But not right now. Anyway, I'm very tired, see, and I'm also disgusted with my job, and I'm nervous as a bastard because I'm worried and I don't worry easy.

ANTONIO. Go on. Don't be temperamental.

PHILIP. He says, that is Max says, and where he is now I wish to hell I knew, that he has a place located, an observation post, you know. Watch them fall, and say it's the wrong place. One of those. Well, he says that the German head of the siege artillery that shells this town comes there and a lovely politician. You know a museum piece. He comes there too. And *Max* thinks. And *I* think he is screwball. But he thinks better. I think *faster,* but he thinks better. That we can bag those citizens. Now listen very carefully, *mi Coronel,* and correct me instantly. *I* think it sounds very romantic. But *Max* says, and he's a German and very practical, and he'd just as soon go behind the fascist lines as you would go to get a shave, or what shall we say. Well *he* says it's perfectly practical. So *I* thought. And I'm sort of drunk now on drinking nothing for so long. That we would sort of suspend the other projects that we have been working on, temporarily, and try to get these two people for you. I don't think the German is of much practical use to you, but he has a very high exchange value indeed, and this project sort of, in a way, appeals to Max. Lay it to nationalism, I say. But if we get this other citizen you've got something, *mi Coronel*. Because he is very, *very* terrific. I mean *terrific*. He, you see, is *outside* the town. But he knows who is *inside* the town. And then you just sort of bring him into good voice and *you* know who is inside the town. Because they all communicate with him. I talk too much, don't I?

ANTONIO. Philip.

PHILIP. Yes, Mi Coronel.

ANTONIO. Philip, now go to Chicote's and get drunk like a good boy and do your work, and come or call when you have news.

PHILIP. And what do I talk, *mi Coronel*, American or English?

ANTONIO. What you like. Do not talk silly. But go now, please, because we are good friends and I like you very much, but I am very busy. Listen, is it true about the observation post?

PHILIP. Yeah.

ANTONIO. What a thing.

PHILIP. Very fancy, though. Awfully, *awfully* fancy, *mi Coronel*.

ANTONIO. Go, please, and start.

PHILIP. And I talk either English or American?

ANTONIO. What's all that about? Go.

PHILIP. Then I'll talk English. Christ, I can lie so much easier in English, it's pitiful.

ANTONIO. GO. GO. GO. GO. GO.

PHILIP. Yes, *mi Coronel*. Thank you for the instructive little talk. I'll go to Chicote's now. *Salud, mi Coronel*.

[*He salutes, looks at his watch and goes*]

ANTONIO. [*At the desk, looks after him. Then rings. Two* ASSAULT GUARDS *come in. They salute*] Now just bring me in that man you took out before. I want to talk to him a little while alone by myself.

CURTAIN

ACT TWO • SCENE TWO

*A corner table at Chicote's bar. It is the first table
on your right as you enter the door. The door and
the window are sandbagged about three quarters
of the way up.* PHILIP *is seated at the table with*
ANITA. *A* WAITER *comes over to the table.*

PHILIP. Any of the barrel whiskey left?

WAITER. Nothing now of the real but gin.

PHILIP. Good gin?

WAITER. The yellow of Booth's. The best.

PHILIP. With bitters.

ANITA. You don't love any more?

PHILIP. No.

ANITA. You make big mistake with that big blonde.

PHILIP. What *big* blonde?

ANITA. That great big blonde. Tall like a tower. Big like a
horse.

PHILIP. Blonde like a wheat field.

ANITA. You make a mistake. Big a woman. Big a mistake.

PHILIP. What makes you think she's so big?

ANITA. Big? Is big like a tank. Wait you get her with a baby.
Big? Is a Studebaker truck.

PHILIP. That's a lovely word, Studebaker, as you say it.

ANITA. Yes. I like best any English word I know. Studebaker.
Is beautiful. Why you no love?

PHILIP. I don't know, Anita. You know. Things change.

[*He looks at his watch*]

ANITA. You use a like fine. Is just the same.

PHILIP. I know it.

ANITA. You like before. You like again. Is must only try.

PHILIP. I know.

ANITA. When is have something good you don't want to go

away. Is a big woman plenty trouble. I know. I been this a long time.

PHILIP. You're a fine girl, Anita.

ANITA. Is on account they all criticize because I bite Mr. Vernon that time?

PHILIP. No. Of course not.

ANITA. I tell you I give a lot not to do that.

PHILIP. Oh, nobody remembers that.

ANITA. You know why I do? Everybody know I bite, but nobody ever ask why.

PHILIP. Why was it?

ANITA. He try to take three hundred pesetas out my stocking. What I should do? Say "Yes, go ahead. All right. Help yourself"? No, I bite.

PHILIP. Quite right, too.

ANITA. You think? Really?

PHILIP. Yes.

ANITA. Oh, you sweet all right. Listen, you don't want make mistake now with that big blonde.

PHILIP. You know, Anita. I'm afraid I do. I'm afraid that's the whole trouble. I want to make an absolutely colossal mistake.

[*He calls the* WAITER, *looks at his watch. To* WAITER]

What time have you?

WAITER. [*Looks at the clock over the bar and at Philip's watch*] The same as you have.

ANITA. Be colossal all right.

PHILIP. You're not jealous?

ANITA. No. I just hate. Last night I try to like. I say hokay everybody a comrade. Comes a big bombardment. Maybe everybody killed. Should be comrades everybody with each other. Bury the axes. Not be selfish. Not be egotistic. Love a enemy like a self. All that slop.

PHILIP. You were terrific.

ANITA. That kind a stuff don't last over the night. This morning I wake up. First thing I do I hate that woman all day long.

PHILIP. You mustn't, you know.

ANITA. What she want with you? She take a man just like you pick a flowers. She don't want. She just pick to put in her room. She just like you because you big, too. Listen. I like you if you was a dwarf.

PHILIP. Na, Anita. No. Be careful.

ANITA. Listen good. I like you if you was sick. I like you if dry up and be ugly. I like you if you hunchback.

PHILIP. Hunchbacks are lucky.

ANITA. I like you if you *unlucky* hunchback. I like you if you got no money. You want? I make it.

PHILIP. That's about the only thing I haven't tried on this job.

ANITA. I not joke. I'm a serious. Philip, you leave her alone. You come back where you know is hokay.

PHILIP. I'm afraid I can't, Anita.

ANITA. You just try. Isn't any change. You like before, you like again. Always works that way when a man is a man.

PHILIP. But you see I change. It's not that I mean to.

ANITA. You no change. I know you good. I know you long time now. You not the kind that change.

PHILIP. All men change.

ANITA. Is not the truth. Is get tired, yes. Is want to go away, yes. Is run around, yes. Is get angry, yes, yes. Is treat bad, yes, plenty. Is change? No. Only is to start different habits. Is a habit is all. Right away is the same with whoever.

PHILIP. I see that. Yes, that's right. But you see it's this sort of running into some one from your own people, and it upsets you.

ANITA. Is not from your own people. Is not like you. Is a different breed of people.

PHILIP. No, it's the same sort of people.

ANITA. Listen, that big blonde make you crazy already. This soon you can't think good. Is no more the same as you as blood and paint. Is look the same. Can a blood. Can a paint. All right. Put the paint in the body, instead of blood. What you get? American woman.

PHILIP. You're unjust to her, Anita. Granted she's lazy and

spoiled, and rather stupid, and enormously on the make. Still she's very beautiful, very friendly, and very charming and rather innocent—and quite brave.

ANITA. Hokay. Beautiful? What you want with beautiful when you're through? I know you. Friendly? Hokay; is friendly can be unfriendly. Charming? Yes. Is a charming like the snake with rabbits. Innocent? You make me laugh. Ha, ha, ha. Is a innocent until a prove the guilty. Brave? Brave? You make me laugh again if I have any laugh left in my belly. Brave? All right. I laugh. Ho, ho, ho. What you do all the time this war you can't tell a ignorance from a brave? Brave? My this——

[*She rises from the table and slaps her behind*]

So. Now I go.

PHILIP. You're awfully hard on her.

ANITA. Hard on her? I like to throw a hand grenade in the bed where she sleeping right this minute. I tell you true. Last night I try all that stuff. All that sacrifice. All that giveup. You know. Now have one good *healthy* feeling. I hate.

[*She goes*]

PHILIP. [*To the* WAITER] You haven't seen a comrade from the International Brigades here asking for me? Name of Max? A comrade with a face sort of broken across here.

[*He puts his hand across his mouth and jaw*]

A comrade with his teeth gone in front? With sort of black gums where they burnt them with a red-hot iron? And with a scar here?

[*He runs his finger across the lower angle of his jaw*]

Have you seen such a comrade?

WAITER. He hasn't been here.

PHILIP. If such a comrade comes, will you ask him to come to the hotel?

WAITER. What hotel?

PHILIP. He'll know what hotel.

[*Starts out and looks back*]

Tell him I went out looking for him.

CURTAIN

ACT TWO • SCENE THREE

*Same as Act I, Scene III. The two adjoining rooms
109 and 110 in the Hotel Florida. It is dark outside
the rooms and the curtains are drawn. There is no
one in room 110 and it is dark. Room 109 is
lighted brightly both by the reading lamp on the
table, the main light in the ceiling, and a reading
lamp clamped to the head of the bed. The electric
heater and the electric stove are both on.* DOROTHY
BRIDGES, *wearing a turtle-neck sweater, a tweed
skirt, wool stockings and jodhpur boots, is doing
something with a long-handled stew-pan on the
electric cooking ring. A distant noise of gun fire
comes through the curtained windows.* DOROTHY
*rings the bell. There is no answering sound. She
rings again.*

DOROTHY. Oh, damn that electrician!

[*She goes to the door and opens it*]

Petra! Oh, Petra!

[*You hear the* MAID *coming down the hall. She comes in
the door*]

PETRA. Yes, Señorita?
DOROTHY. Where's the electrician, Petra?
PETRA. Didn't you know?
DOROTHY. No. What? He's simply got to come and fix this bell!

PETRA. He can't come, Señorita, because he's dead.

DOROTHY. What do you say?

PETRA. He was hit last night when he went out during the bombardment.

DOROTHY. He went out during the bombardment?

PETRA. Yes, Señorita. He had been drinking a little, and he went out to go home.

DOROTHY. The poor little man!

PETRA. Yes, Señorita, it was a shame!

DOROTHY. How was he hit, Petra?

PETRA. Some one shot him from a window, they say. I don't know. That's what they told me.

DOROTHY. Who'd shoot him from a window?

PETRA. Oh, they always shoot from windows at night during a bombardment. The Fifth Column people. The people who fight us from inside the city.

DOROTHY. But why would they shoot him? He was only a poor little workman.

PETRA. They could see he was a workingman from his clothes.

DOROTHY. Of course, Petra.

PETRA. That's why they shot him. They are our enemies. Even of me. If I was killed they would be happy. They would think it was one working person less.

DOROTHY. But it's *dreadful!*

PETRA. Yes, Señorita.

DOROTHY. But it's terrible. You mean they shoot at people that they don't even know who they are?

PETRA. Oh, yes. They are our enemies.

DOROTHY. They're terrible people!

PETRA. Yes, Señorita!

DOROTHY. And what will we do for an *electricista?*

PETRA. Tomorrow we can get another. But now they would all be closed. You should not burn so many lights perhaps, Señorita, and then perhaps the fuse will not melt out. Use only what you need to see.

[DOROTHY *turns off all but the reading light on the bed*]

DOROTHY. Now I can't even see to cook this mess. I suppose that's better though. It didn't say on the tin whether you could heat it or not. It will probably be frightful!

PETRA. What are you cooking, Señorita?

DOROTHY. I don't know, Petra. There wasn't any label on it.

PETRA. [*Peering into the pot*] It looks like rabbit.

DOROTHY. What looks like rabbit is cat. But I don't think they'd bother to put cat up in a tin and ship it all the way from Paris, do you? Of course, they may have tinned it in Barcelona and then shipped it to Paris and then flown it down here. Do you think it's cat, Petra?

PETRA. If it's put up in Barcelona, you can't tell what it is!

DOROTHY. Oh, I'm sick of the whole thing. You go ahead and cook it, Petra!

PETRA. Yes, Señorita. What should I put in?

DOROTHY. [*Picking up a book and going over to the reading light to stretch out on the bed*] Put in anything. Open a tin of anything.

PETRA. Is it for Mr. Philip?

DOROTHY. If he comes.

PETRA. Mr. Philip wouldn't like just anything. It would be better to put in carefully for Mr. Philip. One time he threw a whole breakfast tray on the floor.

DOROTHY. Why, Petra?

PETRA. It was something he read in the paper.

DOROTHY. It was Eden, probably. He hates Eden.

PETRA. Still it was a very violent thing to do. I told him he had no right. *No hay derecho,* I told him.

DOROTHY. And what did he do?

PETRA. He helped me pick it all up, and then he slapped me here when I was bending over. Señorita, I do not like to see him in that next room. He is a different cultural than you.

DOROTHY. I love him, Petra.

PETRA. Señorita! Please do not do such a thing. You haven't

done his room and made his bed for seven months as I have. Señorita, he's *bad*. I do not say he is not a good man. But he is *bad*.

DOROTHY. You mean he's wicked?

PETRA. No. Not wicked. Wicked is dirty. He is very clean. He takes baths all the time even with cold water. Even in the coldest weather he washes his feet. But, Señorita, he is not good. And he will not make you happy.

DOROTHY. But Petra, he made me happier than any one has ever made me.

PETRA. Señorita, that is nothing.

DOROTHY. What do you mean, that's *nothing?*

PETRA. Here everybody can do that!

DOROTHY. You're just a nation of braggarts. Do I have to listen to all that about *conquistadores* and all that?

PETRA. I only meant that is a badness here. A good man has that too, perhaps, yes, a really good man such as I was married to has that. But *all* bad men have that.

DOROTHY. You mean to hear them talk they have it.

PETRA. No. Señorita.

DOROTHY. [*Intrigued*] You mean they really . . . ?

PETRA. [*Sadly*] Yes, Señorita.

DOROTHY. I don't believe a word of it. And you think Mr. Philip is a *really* bad man?

PETRA. [*Earnestly*] Frightful!

DOROTHY. Oh, I *wonder* where he is?

[*There is a noise of heavy boots coming down the corridor.* PHILIP *and* THREE COMRADES *in I.B. uniform enter* 110, *and* PHILIP *switches on the light.* PHILIP *is bareheaded, wet, and dishevelled looking. One of the* COMRADES *is* MAX, *the one with the broken face. He is covered with mud and as they come into the room, he sits down on a chair before the table, facing the back of the chair, and resting his hands and his chin on the top of the back of the chair. He has an amazing face. One of the other* COMRADES *has a short automatic rifle slung over his shoulder. The other has a long Mauser parabellum pistol in a wooden holster strapped to his leg.*]

PHILIP. I want you to block these two rooms off the corridor. Any one to see me *you* bring them in. How many comrades have you below?

The COMRADE *with the rifle.* Twenty-five.

PHILIP. Here are the keys to room one o eight and one eleven.

[*He hands one to each*]

Have the doors open and stand just inside the door, so you can watch the corridor. No, better get a chair apiece and sit inside the door where you can watch. All right. Get along. . . . Comrades!

[THEY *salute and go out.* PHILIP *goes over to the broken-faced* COMRADE. *He puts his hand on his shoulder. The audience has seen for several moments that he is asleep, but* PHILIP *does not know it*]

PHILIP. Max.

[MAX *wakes, looks at* PHILIP *and smiles*]

Was it very bad, Max?

[MAX *looks at him and smiles again and shakes his head*]

MAX. *Nicht zu schwer.*
PHILIP. And when comes he?
MAX. In the evenings of grand bombardment.
PHILIP. And where?
MAX. To the roof of a house at the top of Extremadura road. It has a little tower.
PHILIP. I thought he came to Garabitas.
MAX. So did I.
PHILIP. And when gives more grand bombardment?
MAX. Tonight.
PHILIP. When?
MAX. *Fiertel nach zwölf.*

PHILIP. You're sure?

MAX. You should see the shells. Everything all laid out. Also they are very sloppy soldiers. If I did not have this face I could have stayed and worked a gun. Maybe they put me on the staff even.

PHILIP. Where did you change the uniform? I was out there looking for you at a couple of places.

MAX. In one of the houses in Carabanchel. There are a hundred to pick from in that stretch that no one holds. A hundred and four, I think. Between our lines and theirs. Over there it was all right. The soldiers are all young. It was only if an officer should see my face. An officer would know where these faces come from.

PHILIP. So now?

MAX. I think we go tonight. Why wait?

PHILIP. How is it?

MAX. Muddy.

PHILIP. How many do you need?

MAX. You and me. Or whoever you send with me.

PHILIP. Me.

MAX. Good! Now how is it to take a bath?

PHILIP. Fine! Go ahead.

MAX. And I sleep a little while.

PHILIP. What time should we leave?

MAX. By half past nine.

PHILIP. Get some sleep then.

MAX. You call me?

[*He goes into the bathroom.* PHILIP *goes out of the room, closes the door, and knocks on the door of* 109]

DOROTHY. [*From the bed*] Come in!

PHILIP. Hello, darling.

DOROTHY. Hello.

PHILIP. Are you cooking?

DOROTHY. I was, but I got bored with it. Are you hungry?

PHILIP. Famished.

DOROTHY. It's in the pot there. Turn on the stove and it will warm up.

PHILIP. What's the matter with you, Bridges?

DOROTHY. Where have you been?

PHILIP. Just out in the town.

DOROTHY. Doing what?

PHILIP. Just around.

DOROTHY. You've left me alone all day. Ever since that poor man was shot in there this morning you've left me alone. I've waited in here the whole day. No one's even been to see me all day except Preston and he was so unpleasant I had to ask him to leave. Where have you been?

PHILIP. Just around and about.

DOROTHY. Chicote's?

PHILIP. Yes.

DOROTHY. And did you see that horrible Moor?

PHILIP. Oh, yes, Anita. She sent messages.

DOROTHY. She's unspeakable! You can keep the messages.

[PHILIP *has ladled some of the contents of the stew-pan onto a plate and tastes it*]

PHILIP. I say. What is this?

DOROTHY. I don't know.

PHILIP. I say. It's jolly good. Did you cook it yourself?

DOROTHY. [*Coyly*] Yes. Do you like it?

PHILIP. I didn't know you could cook.

DOROTHY. [*Shyly*] Really, Philip?

PHILIP. I say it *is* good! But what gave you the idea of putting kippers in it?

DOROTHY. Oh, damn Petra! So that was the other tin she opened.

[*There is a knock on the door. It is the* MANAGER. *One of his arms is firmly held by the* COMRADE *with the automatic rifle*]

RIFLE COMRADE. This comrade here said he wanted to see you.

PHILIP. Thank you, Comrade. Let him come in.

[*The* RIFLE COMRADE *turns the* MANAGER *loose and salutes*]

MANAGER. It was an absolutely nothing, Mr. Philip. Passing in hall with overkeenness of smell produced by hunger, detected odor of cooking and stopped. Instantly was seized by the comrade. Perfectly all right, Mr. Philip. Absolutely nothing. Do not concern yourself. *Buen provecho,* Mr. Philip. Eat well, Madame.

PHILIP. You came by just at the right moment. I have something for you. Take this.

[*Hands him the casserole, the plate, the fork, and ladle, with both hands*]

MANAGER. Mr. Philip. No. I cannot.

PHILIP. Comrade Stamp Collector, you must!

MANAGER. No, Mr. Philip.

[*Taking them*]

I cannot. You move me to the tears. I could never. It is too much!

PHILIP. Comrade, not a word more!

MANAGER. You dissolve my heart in feeling. Mr. Philip, from my heart his bottom, I thank you.

[*He goes out, holding the plate in one hand, the stew-pan in the other*]

DOROTHY. Philip, I'm sorry.

PHILIP. If you don't mind, I'll take a little whiskey with plain water. Then you might open a tin of the bully beef and slice up an onion.

DOROTHY. But Philip, darling, I can't bear the smell of onions!

PHILIP. Chances are that won't bother us tonight.

DOROTHY. You mean you're not going to be here?

PHILIP. I have to go out.

DOROTHY. Why?

PHILIP. With the boys.

DOROTHY. I know what that means.

PHILIP. Do you?

DOROTHY. Yes. Only too well.

PHILIP. Ghastly, isn't it?

DOROTHY. It's hateful! The whole way you waste your time and your life is hateful and stupid.

PHILIP. And me so young and promising.

DOROTHY. You're nasty to go out tonight when we could stay and have a lovely evening like last night.

PHILIP. It's the beast in me.

DOROTHY. But Philip, you could stay here. You can drink right here or do anything you want. I'll be gay and play the phonograph. I'll drink too, even if it gives me a headache afterwards. We'll get a lot of people in if you want a lot of people. It can be noisy and full of smoke, and everything you like. You don't have to go out, Philip!

PHILIP. Come here and kiss me!

[*He holds her in his arms*]

DOROTHY. And don't eat onions, Philip. If you don't eat the onions, I'll feel surer of you.

PHILIP. All right. I won't eat the onions. Have you any tomato catsup?

[*There is a knock at the door. It is the* RIFLE COMRADE *again with the* MANAGER]

RIFLE COMRADE. This comrade back here again!

PHILIP. Thank you, Comrade. Let him in.

[RIFLE COMRADE *salutes and goes out*]

MANAGER. Is just come tell you all right can take a joke, Mr. Philip. Is a sense of humor O.K.

[*Sadly*]

Is a food right now not to joke with. Neither is to spoil, maybe, if you think it over. But is all right. I take the joke.

PHILIP. Take a couple of tins of this.

[*He gives him two tins of corned beef from the armoire*]

DOROTHY. Whose beef is that?

PHILIP. Oh, I suppose it's your beef.

MANAGER. Thank you, Mr. Philip. Is a good joke all right. Ha, ha. Expensive all right, yes, maybe. But thank you, Mr. Philip. Thank *you*, too, Miss.

[*He goes out*]

PHILIP. Look, Bridges.

[*He puts his arms around her*]

Don't mind me if I'm stuffy tonight.

DOROTHY. Darling, all I want is for you to stay in. I want us to have some sort of home-life. It's nice here. I could fix up your room and make it attractive.

PHILIP. It got a touch messy this morning.

DOROTHY. I'd fix it up so you'd like it to live in. You could have a comfortable chair and a bookcase, and a good reading light, and pictures. I could fix it really nicely. Please stay here tonight and just see how nice it is.

PHILIP. Tomorrow night.

DOROTHY. Why not tonight, darling?

PHILIP. Oh, tonight's one of those restless nights when you feel you have to get out and buzz around and see people. And, besides, I have an appointment.

DOROTHY. At what time?

PHILIP. At a quarter past twelve.

DOROTHY. Then come back afterwards.

PHILIP. All right.

DOROTHY. Come in any time.

PHILIP. Really——?

DOROTHY. Yes. Please.

[*He takes her in his arms. He strokes her hair. Tips her head back and kisses her. There is noise of shouting and singing downstairs. Then you hear the* COMRADES *break into "The Partizan." They sing it all the way through*]

DOROTHY. That's a lovely song.

PHILIP. You'll never know how fine a song that is.

[*The* COMRADES *are singing "Bandera Rosa"*]

PHILIP. You know this one?

[*He sits by her now on the bed*]

DOROTHY. Yes.

PHILIP. The best people I ever knew died for that song.

[*In the next room you can see the broken-faced* COMRADE *asleep. While they have been talking, he finished his bath, dried his clothes, knocked the mud off them, and lay down on the bed. As he sleeps, the light shines on his face*]

DOROTHY. [*Beside Philip, on the bed*] Philip, Philip, please, Philip!

PHILIP. You know I don't feel so much like making love tonight.

DOROTHY. [*Disappointed*] That's fine. That's lovely! But I'd only like to have you stay here. Just stay in and have a little home-life.

PHILIP. I have to go, you know. Really.

[*Downstairs the* COMRADES *are singing the "Comintern" song*]

DOROTHY. That's the one they always play at funerals.

PHILIP. They sing it at other times, though.

DOROTHY. Philip, please don't go!

PHILIP. [*Holding her in his arms*] Good-bye.

DOROTHY. No. Please, please, don't go!

PHILIP. [*Standing up*] Look, open both the windows before you go to bed, will you? You don't want to have any glass broken if there's a shelling around midnight.

DOROTHY. Don't go, Philip. Please don't go!

PHILIP. Salud, Camarada!

[*He does not salute. He goes into the next room. Downstairs the* COMRADES *are singing the "Partizan" again.* PHILIP, *in 110, looks at* MAX *sleeping; then goes over to wake him*]

Max!

[MAX, *waking instantly, looks around him, blinks at the light in his eyes, then smiles*]

MAX. Is time?

PHILIP. Yes. Want a drink?

MAX. [*Getting up from the bed, smiling, and feeling of his boots, which have been drying in front of the electric heater*] Very much.

[PHILIP *pours two whiskeys and reaches for the water bottle*]

Do not spoil it with water.

PHILIP. Salud!

MAX. Salud!

PHILIP. Let's go.

CURTAIN

[*Downstairs the* COMRADES *are singing the "International." As the curtain comes down,* DOROTHY BRIDGES *is on the bed in Room 109, with her arms around the pillows; and her shoulders shaking as she is crying*]

ACT TWO • SCENE FOUR

Same as Scene III, but four thirty o'clock in the morning. Both rooms are dark and DOROTHY BRIDGES *is asleep in her bed.* MAX *and* PHILIP *come*

down the corridor, and PHILIP *unlocks the door of*
Room 110 and switches on the light. They look at
each other. MAX *shakes his head. They are both so*
covered with mud that they are almost unrecog-
nizable.

PHILIP. Well, another time.

MAX. I am very sorry.

PHILIP. It's not your fault. Want to bathe first?

MAX. [*His head on his arms*] Go ahead and take it. I am too
tired.

[PHILIP *goes into the bathroom. Then comes out*]

PHILIP. There's no hot water. Only reason we live in this
damn death trap is for hot water, and now there's none!

MAX. [*Very sleepily*] I am very sad to fail. I was certain they
were coming. But they did not come.

PHILIP. Get your clothes off, and get some sleep. You're a marvellous bloody damned scout officer, and you know it. Nobody
could do what you've done . . . it's not your fault if they call off
the shoot.

MAX. [*Really utterly and completely exhausted*] I am too
sleepy. I am so sleepy I am sick.

PHILIP. Come on, I'll get you to bed.

[*He pulls his boots off and helps him to undress.* PHILIP
tumbles him into bed]

MAX. The bed is good.

[*He takes hold of the pillow with his arms and spreads his*
legs wide]

I sleep on my face, and then it does not frighten anybody in the
morning.

PHILIP. [*From the bathroom*] Take the whole bed. I'm bunk-
ing in another room.

[PHILIP *goes into the bathroom and you hear him splashing. He comes out in pajamas and a dressing gown, opens the door connecting the two rooms, ducks under the poster and goes over to the bed and climbs in*]

DOROTHY. [*In the dark*] Darling, is it late?

PHILIP. Fiveish.

DOROTHY. [*Very sleepily*] Where have you been?

PHILIP. On a visit.

DOROTHY. [*Who is still really asleep*] Did you keep your appointment?

PHILIP. [*Rolling away to one side of the bed so that he is back to back with her*] The man didn't show up.

DOROTHY. [*Very sleepily, but anxious to impart news*] There wasn't any shelling, darling.

PHILIP. Good!

DOROTHY. Good night, darling.

PHILIP. Good night!

[*You hear a machine-gun go pop-pop-pop a long way away through the open window. They lie very quietly in the bed and then we hear* PHILIP *say*]

Bridges, are you asleep?

DOROTHY. [*Really asleep*] No, darling. Not if——

PHILIP. I want to tell you something.

DOROTHY. [*Sleepily*] Yes, my very dear.

PHILIP. I want to tell you two things. I've got the horrors, and I love you.

DOROTHY. Oh, you poor Philip.

PHILIP. I never tell anybody when I get the horrors, and I never tell anybody I love them. But I love you, see? Do you hear me? Do you feel me? Do you hear me say it?

DOROTHY. Why, I love you all the time. And you feel lovely. Sort of like a snow storm if snow wasn't cold and didn't melt.

PHILIP. I don't love you in the daytime. I don't love anything in the daytime. Listen, I want to say something else. Would you like to marry me or stay with me all the time or go wherever I go, and be my girl? Hear me say it? I said it, see.

DOROTHY. Darling, I'd like to *marry* you.

PHILIP. Yeah. I say funny things in the night, don't I?

DOROTHY. I'd like us to be married and work hard and have a fine life. You know I'm not as silly as I sound, or I wouldn't be here. And I work when you're not around. And just because I can't cook. You can hire people to cook under normal circumstances. Oh, you. I love you with the big shoulders and the walk like a gorilla and the funny face.

PHILIP. It'll be a lot funnier face when I get through with this business.

DOROTHY. Are the horrors any better, darling? Do you want to tell me about them?

PHILIP. Oh, the hell with them. I've had them so long I'd miss them if they went away. Let me say one thing more to you.

[*He says it very slowly*]

I'd like to marry you, and go away, and get out of all this. Did I say it just like that? Did you hear me say it?

DOROTHY. Well, darling, we will.

PHILIP. No, we won't. Even lying in the night I know we won't. But I like to say it. Oh, I love you. Goddamn it, goddamn it, I love you. And you've got the loveliest damn body in the world. And I adore you, too. Did you hear me say that?

DOROTHY. Yes, my sweet, but it's not true about my body. It's just an all right body, but I like to hear you say it. And tell me about the horrors, and maybe they will go away.

PHILIP. No. Everybody gets their own, and you don't want to pass them around.

DOROTHY. Should we try to go to sleep, my big lovely one? My old snow storm.

PHILIP. It's getting almost daylight, and I'm getting sensible again.

DOROTHY. Please try to go to sleep.

PHILIP. Listen, Bridges, while I say something else. It's getting light now.

DOROTHY. [*Her voice catching*] Yes, darling.

PHILIP. If you want me to go to sleep, Bridges, just hit me on the head with a hammer.

CURTAIN

END OF ACT TWO

ACT THREE • SCENE ONE

TIME: *Five days later. It is afternoon in the same two rooms in the Hotel Florida, 109 and 110.*

The scene is the same as Scene III, Act II except that the door is open between the two rooms. The poster flaps open at the bottom in PHILIP'S *room, on the night table by the bed, there is a vase full of chrysanthemums. There is a bookcase along the wall to the right of the bed, and cretonne covers on the chairs. There are curtains on the windows, of the same cretonne, and the bed has a cover over its white spread. All clothes are hung neatly on hangers, and three pairs of* PHILIP'S *boots, all brushed and polished, are being put into the closet by* PETRA. DOROTHY *in the next room, 109, is trying on a silver fox cape before the mirror.*

DOROTHY. Petra, please come here!
PETRA. [*Straightening her little and old body up from putting the boots away*] Yes, Señorita!

[PETRA *goes around and comes in by the proper door to 109, knocking as she opens it*]

PETRA. [*Holding her hands together*] Oh, Señorita, it's beautiful!
DOROTHY. [*Looking over her shoulder into the mirror*] It's not right, Petra. I don't know *what* they've done, but it's *not* right!
PETRA. It looks lovely, Señorita!
DOROTHY. No, there's something wrong with the top of the

collar. And I can't speak Spanish well enough to explain to that fool of a furrier. He *is* a fool.

[*You hear some one coming down the hall. It is* PHILIP. *He opens the door to* 110 *and looks around. He takes off his leather coat, and tosses it onto the bed, then sails his beret toward the clothes-rack in the corner. It falls on the floor. He sits down on one of the cretonne-covered chairs, and pulls his boots off. He leaves them standing, dripping, in the middle of the floor and goes over to the bed. He picks up his coat from the bed and throws it onto a chair. It sprawls there. Then he lies down on the bed, pulls the pillows out from under the cover to make a pile under his head, and turns on the reading light. He reaches down, opens the double door of the night table, by the bed, gets out a bottle of whiskey, pours himself a drink into the glass which had been placed neatly, top down, on top of the water bottle, and splashes water into it. With the glass in his left hand, he reaches over to the bookcase for a book. He lies back a moment, still, then shrugs his shoulders and twists uncomfortably. Finally, he brings a pistol out from underneath his belt band and lays it on the bedcover beside him. He draws his knees up, takes his first sip of the drink, and commences to read*]

DOROTHY. [*From the next room*] Philip, Philip darling!

PHILIP. Yes.

DOROTHY. Come in here, please.

PHILIP. No, dear.

DOROTHY. I want to show you something.

PHILIP. [*Reading*] Bring it in here.

DOROTHY. All right, darling.

[*She takes a last look at the cape in the mirror. She is very beautiful in it, and there is nothing wrong with the neck. She comes in the door wearing the cape very proudly, and turns with it, wearing it very gracefully and elegantly as a model would*]

PHILIP. Where did you get that?

DOROTHY. I bought it, darling.

PHILIP. What with?

DOROTHY. Pesetas.

PHILIP. [*Coldly*] Very pretty.

DOROTHY. Don't you like it?

PHILIP. [*Still staring at the cape*] Very pretty.

DOROTHY. What's the matter, Philip?

PHILIP. Nothing.

DOROTHY. Don't you want me to have *anything* nice-looking?

PHILIP. That's absolutely your affair.

DOROTHY. But, *darling.* It's so cheap. The foxes only cost twelve hundred pesetas apiece.

PHILIP. That's one hundred and twenty days' pay for a man in the brigades. Let's see. That's four months. I don't believe I know any one who's been out four months without being hit—or killed.

DOROTHY. But, Philip, it doesn't have anything to do with the brigades. I bought pesetas at fifty to the dollar in Paris.

PHILIP. [*Coldly*] Really?

DOROTHY. Yes, darling. And why shouldn't I buy foxes if I want to? Some one has to buy them. They're there to be sold, and they come to less than twenty-two dollars a skin.

PHILIP. Marvellous, isn't it? How many foxes are there?

DOROTHY. About twelve. Oh, Philip, don't be cross.

PHILIP. You're doing quite well out of the war, aren't you? How did you smuggle your pesetas in?

DOROTHY. In a tin of Mum.

PHILIP. Mum, oh, yes, Mum. Mum's the word. And did the Mum take all the odor off them?

DOROTHY. Philip, you're acting *frightfully* moral!

PHILIP. I suppose I am frightfully moral, economically. I don't think even Mum, or what's the other lovely thing ladies use, Amolin is it?, would take the taint off those Black Bourse pesetas.

DOROTHY. If you're going to be unpleasant about it, I'll leave you.

PHILIP. Good!

[DOROTHY *starts out of the room, but turns at the door pleadingly*]

DOROTHY. But don't be unpleasant about it. Just be reasonable, and be pleased that I have such a lovely cape. Do you know what I was doing when you came in? I was thinking what we could do at just this time of day in Paris.

PHILIP. Paris?

DOROTHY. It will just be getting dark, and I meet you at the Ritz bar, and I'm wearing this cape. I'm sitting there waiting for you. You come in wearing a double-breasted guardsman's overcoat, very close fitting, a bowler hat, and you're carrying a stick.

PHILIP. You've been reading that American magazine, *Esquire*. You're not supposed to read what it says, you know. You're only supposed to look at the pictures.

DOROTHY. You order a whiskey with Perrier, and I have a champagne cocktail.

PHILIP. I don't like it.

DOROTHY. What?

PHILIP. The story. If you have to have day dreams, just keep me out of them, will you?

DOROTHY. It's just *playing,* darling.

PHILIP. Well, I don't play any more.

DOROTHY. But you did, darling. And we had lovely fun playing.

PHILIP. Just count me out now.

DOROTHY. But aren't we friends?

PHILIP. Oh, yes, you make all sorts of friends in a war.

DOROTHY. Darling, *please* stop it! Aren't we lovers?

PHILIP. Oh, that? Oh, certainly. Of course. Why not?

DOROTHY. But aren't we going to go and live together and have a lovely time and be happy? The way you say always in the night?

PHILIP. No. Not in a hundred thousand bloody years. Never believe what I say in the night. I lie like hell at night.

DOROTHY. But *why* can't we do what you say we'll do at night?

PHILIP. Because I'm in something where you don't go on and live together and have a lovely time and be happy.

DOROTHY. But why not?

PHILIP. Because, principally, I've discovered you're too busy. And secondly, it doesn't seem very important compared to any number of other things.

DOROTHY. But you're *never* busy!

PHILIP. [*He feels himself talking too much, but goes on*] No. But after this is over I'll get a course of discipline to rid me of any anarchistic habits I may have acquired. I'll probably be sent back to working with pioneers or something like that.

DOROTHY. I don't understand.

PHILIP. And because you don't understand, and you never could understand, is the reason we're not going to go on and live together and have a lovely time and etcetera.

DOROTHY. Oh, it's worse than Skull and Bones.

PHILIP. What in God's name is Skull and Bones?

DOROTHY. It's a secret society a man belonged to one time that I had just enough sense not to marry. It's very superior and awfully good and worthy, and they take you in and tell you all about it, just before the wedding, and when they told me about it, I called the wedding off.

PHILIP. That's an excellent precedent.

DOROTHY. But can't we just go on now, as long as we have each other, I mean if we aren't going to always keep on, and be nice and enjoy what we have and not be bitter?

PHILIP. If you like.

DOROTHY. I'd like.

[*She has come over from the door and is standing by the bed while they have been talking.* PHILIP *looks up at her, then stands up, takes her in his arms and lifts her against him onto the bed, silver foxes and all*]

PHILIP. They feel very fine and soft.

DOROTHY. They don't smell badly, do they?

PHILIP. [*His face over her shoulder in the foxes*] No, they don't smell badly. And you feel lovely in them. And I love you, I don't give a damn. I do. And it's only half-past five in the afternoon.

DOROTHY. And while we have it we can have it, can't we?

PHILIP. [*Shamelessly*] They feel really marvellously. I'm glad you bought them.

[*He holds her very close*]

DOROTHY. We can have it now just this little while that we have?

PHILIP. Yes. We'll have it.

[*There is a knock on the door and the handle turns to admit* MAX. PHILIP *gets off the bed.* DOROTHY *remains seated on it*]

MAX. I disturb? Yes?

PHILIP. No. Not at all. Max, this is an American comrade. Comrade Bridges. Comrade Max.

MAX. Salud, Comrade.

[*He goes over to the bed where* DOROTHY *is still seated and puts out his hand.* DOROTHY *shakes it and looks away*]

MAX. You are busy? Yes?

PHILIP. No. Not at all. Will you have a drink, Max?

MAX. No. Thank you.

PHILIP. ¿Hay novedades?

MAX. *Algunas.*

PHILIP. You won't have a drink?

MAX. No. Thank you very much.

DOROTHY. I'll go. Don't let me bother you.

PHILIP. There's no need to go.

DOROTHY. You'll come by later, perhaps.

PHILIP. Quite.

[*As she goes out* MAX *says with great politeness*]

MAX. Salud, Camarada.

DOROTHY. Salud.

[*She shuts the door between the two rooms before she goes out the regular door*]

MAX. [*When they are alone*] She is a Comrade?

PHILIP. No.

MAX. You introduced her as so.

PHILIP. Just a manner of speech. You call every one comrade in Madrid. All supposed to be working for the same cause.

MAX. It is not such a good manner of speech.

PHILIP. No. I suppose not. I seem to remember saying something like that myself once.

MAX. This girl, how do you call her? Britches?

PHILIP. Bridges.

MAX. She is something serious to you?

PHILIP. Serious?

MAX. Yes. You know what I mean.

PHILIP. I wouldn't say so. You could call her comic, rather. In some ways.

MAX. You spend much time with her?

PHILIP. A certain amount.

MAX. Whose time?

PHILIP. My time.

MAX. Never the Party's time?

PHILIP. My time is the Party's time.

MAX. That is what I mean. I am glad you understand so easily.

PHILIP. Oh, I understand very easily.

MAX. Do not be angry about something that is not you nor me.

PHILIP. I'm not angry. But I'm not supposed to be a damn monk.

MAX. Philip, Comrade. You have never been much like a damned monk.

PHILIP. No?

MAX. Nor does anybody expect you to be—ever.

PHILIP. No.

MAX. It is only a question of what interferes with your work. This girl—where does she come from? What is her background?

PHILIP. Ask her.

MAX. I suppose I will have to, then.

PHILIP. Haven't I done my work properly? Has any one complained?

MAX. Not until now.

PHILIP. And who complains now?

MAX. I complain now.

PHILIP. Yes?

MAX. Yes. I should have met you at Chicote's. If you were not there you should have left word for me. I go to Chicote's on time. You are not there. There is no word. I come here and find you with 'ner ganzen menagerie of silver foxes in your arms.

PHILIP. And you never want any of that?

MAX. Oh, yes. I want it all the time.

PHILIP. And what do *you* do?

MAX. Sometimes when I have time and I am not too tired, I find some one that will give me a little something while she looks the other way.

PHILIP. And you want it all the time?

MAX. I like very much. I am not a saint.

PHILIP. There *are* saints.

MAX. Yes. And others that are not. Only I am always very busy. Now we will talk of something else. Tonight we go again.

PHILIP. Good.

MAX. You want to go?

PHILIP. Look, I agree with you on the girl if you like; but don't be insulting to me. Don't get superior about work.

MAX. This girl is all right?

PHILIP. Oh, quite! She may be bad for me and I may waste time as you say and all that, but she's absolutely straight.

MAX. You are sure? You must remember I have never seen so many foxes.

PHILIP. She's a damned fool and all that, but she's as straight as I am!

MAX. And you are still straight?

PHILIP. I hope so. Does it show when you're not?

MAX. Oh, yes.

PHILIP. How do I look then?

[*He stands and looks at himself contemptuously in the glass.* MAX *looks at him and smiles very slowly. He nods his head*]

MAX. You look pretty straight to me.

PHILIP. You want to go in and question her about her background and all that?

MAX. No.

PHILIP. She has the same background all American girls have that come to Europe with a certain amount of money. They're all the same. Camps, college, money in family, now more or less than it was, usually less now, men, affairs, abortions, ambitions, and finally marry and settle down or don't marry and settle down. They open shops, or work in shops, some write, others play instruments, some go on the stage, some into films. They have something called the Junior League I believe that the virgins work at. All for the public good. This one writes. Quite well too, when she's not too lazy. Ask her about it all if you like. It's very dull though, I tell you.

MAX. I am not interested.

PHILIP. I thought you were.

MAX. No. I think it over and I leave it all to you.

PHILIP. All what to me?

MAX. All about this girl. To deal with as you should.

PHILIP. I wouldn't have too much confidence in me.

MAX. I have confidence in you.

PHILIP. [*Bitterly*] I wouldn't have too much. Sometimes I'm damned tired of it. Of the whole damned business. So I hate it.

MAX. Of course.

PHILIP. Yes. And now you'll talk me out of it. I murdered that bloody young Wilkinson the other day. Just through carelessness. Don't tell me I didn't.

MAX. Now you talk nonsense. But you were not as careful as you should have been.

PHILIP. It was my fault he was killed. I left him in there in the room in my chair with the door open. That wasn't where I was going to use him.

MAX. You did not leave him there on purpose. You must not think about it now that it is over.

PHILIP. No—just a deathtrap set from carelessness.

MAX. He would probably have been killed later anyway.

PHILIP. Oh, yes. Of course. That makes it marvellous, doesn't it? That's perfectly splendid. I suppose I didn't know that, either.

MAX. I have seen you in such a mood before. I know you will be all right again.

PHILIP. Yes. But you know how I'll be when I'm all right? I'll have a dozen drinks in me and I'll be with some tart. Very jolly I'll be. That's your idea of all right with me.

MAX. No.

PHILIP. I'm fed up with it. You know where I'd like to be? At some place like Saint-Tropez on the Riviera, waking up in the morning with no bloody war, and a café crème with proper milk in it . . . and *brioches* with fresh strawberry jam, and *œufs au jambon* all on one tray.

MAX. And the girl?

PHILIP. Yes, and the girl, too. You're damned right, the girl. Silver foxes and all.

MAX. I told you she was bad for you.

PHILIP. Or good for me. I've been doing this so long I'm bloody well fed up with it. With all of it.

MAX. You do it so *every one* will have a good breakfast like that. You do it so *no one* will ever be hungry. You do it so men will not have to fear ill health or old age; so they can live and work in dignity and not as slaves.

PHILIP. Yes. Sure. I know.

MAX. You know why you do it. And if you have a little *défaillance* I understand.

PHILIP. This one was a pretty big *défaillance*, and I've had it a long time. Ever since I saw the girl. You don't know what they do to you.

[*There is the incoming scream of a shell and the sound of its burst in the street. You hear a child scream; first high, then in short, sharp, thin cries. You hear people running in the street. Another shell comes in.* PHILIP *has opened the windows wide. After the burst you hear the sound of people running again*]

MAX. You do it to stop *that* forever.

PHILIP. The swine! They timed it for the minute the cinemas are out.

[*Another shell comes in and bursts, and you hear a dog go yelping down the street*]

MAX. You hear? You do it for all men. You do it for the children. And sometimes you do it even for dogs. Go in and see the girl a while now. She needs you now.

PHILIP. No. Let her take it by herself. She's got her silver foxes. The hell with it all.

MAX. No. Go in now. She needs you now.

[*Another shell comes in with a long swishing rush, and bursts outside in the street. There is no running and no noise after this one*]

MAX. I lie down now for a while here. Go in to her now.

PHILIP. All right. Sure. Anything you say. I do whatever you say.

[*He starts for the door and opens it as there is another inrushing, down-dropping, whishing sound and another burst; beyond the hotel this time*]

MAX. It is just a little bombardment. The big one is for tonight.

[PHILIP *opens the door of the other room. Through the door you hear* PHILIP *speak, in a flat voice*]

PHILIP. Hello, Bridges. How are you?

CURTAIN

ACT THREE • SCENE TWO

Interior of an artillery observation post in a shelled house on the top of the Extremadura road.

It is located in the tower of what has been a very pretentious house and access to it is by a ladder which replaces the circular iron stairway which has been smashed and hangs, broken and twisted. You see the ladder against the tower and at its top, the back of the observation post which faces toward Madrid. It is night and the sacks which plug its windows have been removed and looking out through them you see nothing but darkness because the lights of Madrid have been extinguished. There are large-scale military maps on the walls with the positions marked with colored tacks and tapes, and on a plain table there is a field telephone. There is an extra large size, single, German model, long tube telemeter opposite the narrow opening in the wall to the right of the table and a chair beside it. There is an ordinary-sized double tube telemeter at the other opening with a chair at its base. There is another plain table with a telephone on the right of the room. At the foot of the ladder is a SENTRY *with fixed bayonet, and at the top of the ladder in the room, where there is just enough height for him to stand straight with his rifle and bayonet, there is another* SENTRY. *As the curtain rises, you see the scene as described with the* TWO SENTRIES *at their posts.* Two SIGNALLERS *are bending over the larger table. After the curtain is up, you see the lights of a motor which shine brightly on the ladder at the base of the tower. They come closer and closer and almost blind the* SENTRY.

SENTRY. Cut those lights!

[*The lights shine on, illuminating the* SENTRY *with a blinding light*]

SENTRY. [*Presenting his rifle, pulling back the bolt, and shoving it forward with a click*] Cut those lights!

[*He says it very slowly, clearly and dangerously, and it is obvious that he will fire. The lights go off and* THREE MEN, *two of them in officer's uniform, one large and stout, the other rather thin and elegantly dressed, with riding boots which shine in the flashlight the stout man carries, and a* CIVILIAN, *cross the stage from the left where they have left the motor car off stage; and approach the ladder*]

SENTRY. [*Giving the first half of the password*] The Victory——
THIN OFFICER. [*Snappily and disdainfully*] To those who deserve it.
SENTRY. Pass.
THIN OFFICER. [*To* CIVILIAN] Just climb up here.
CIVILIAN. I've been here before.

[*The three of them climb the ladder. At the top of the ladder the* SENTRY, *seeing the insignia on the cap of the large, stout officer, presents arms. The* SIGNALLERS *remain seated at their telephones. The large officer goes over to the table followed by the* CIVILIAN *and the shiny-booted officer who is obviously his* AIDE]

LARGE OFFICER. What's the matter with these signallers?
AIDE. [*To* SIGNALLERS] Come along! Stand to attention there! What's the matter with you?

[SIGNALLERS *stand to attention rather wearily*]

At ease!

[*The* SIGNALLERS *sit down. The* LARGE OFFICER *is studying the map. The* CIVILIAN *looks out of the telemeter and sees nothing in the darkness*]

CIVILIAN. The bombardment's for midnight?

AIDE. What time is the shoot for, Sir?

[*Speaking to the* LARGE OFFICER]

LARGE OFFICER. [*Speaking with a German accent*] You talk too much!

AIDE. I'm sorry, sir. Would you care to have a look at these?

[*He hands him a sheaf of typed orders clipped together.* LARGE OFFICER *takes them and glances at them. Hands them back*]

LARGE OFFICER. [*In heavy voice*] I am familiar with them. I wrote them.

AIDE. Quite, sir. I thought perhaps you wished to verify them.

LARGE OFFICER. I heff verified them!

[*One of the phones rings.* SIGNALLER *at table takes it and listens*]

SIGNALLER. Yes. No. Yes. All right.

[*He nods to the* LARGE OFFICER]

For you, sir.

[LARGE OFFICER *takes the phone*]

LARGE OFFICER. Hello. Yes. That is right. Are you a fool? No? As ordered. By salvos means by salvos.

[*He hangs up the receiver and looks at his watch*]
[*To* AIDE]

What time have you?

AIDE. Twelve minus one, sir.

LARGE OFFICER. I deal with fools here. You cannot say that you command where there is no discipline. Signallers who sit at table when a General comes in. Artillery brigadiers who ask for explanations of orders. What time did you say it was?

AIDE. [*Looking at his watch*] Twelve minus thirty seconds, sir.

SIGNALLER. The brigade called six times, sir!

LARGE OFFICER. [*Lighting a cigar*] What time?

AIDE. Minus fifteen, sir.

LARGE OFFICER. What minus fifteen what?

AIDE. Twelve minus fifteen seconds, sir.

[*Just then you hear the guns. They are a very different sound from the incoming shells. There is a sharp, cracking boom, boom, boom, boom, as a kettle drum would make struck sharply before a microphone and then whish, whish, whish, whish, chu, chu, chu, chu, chu—chu—as the shells go away followed by a distant burst. Another battery closer and louder commences firing and then they are firing all along the line in quick, pounding thuds and the air is full of the noise the departing projectiles make. Through the open window you see the skyline of Madrid lit now by the flashes. The LARGE OFFICER is standing at the big telemeter. The CIVILIAN at the two-branched one. The AIDE is looking over the CIVILIAN's shoulder*]

CIVILIAN. God, what a beautiful sight!

AIDE. We'll kill plenty of them tonight. The Marxist bastards. This catches them in their holes.

CIVILIAN. It's wonderful to see it.

GENERAL. Is it satisfactory?

[*He does not remove his eyes from the telemeter*]

CIVILIAN. It's beautiful! How long will it go on?

GENERAL. We're giving them an hour. Then ten minutes without. Then fifteen minutes more.

CIVILIAN. No shells will light in the Salamanca quarter, will they? That's where nearly all our people are.

GENERAL. A few will land there.

CIVILIAN. But why?

GENERAL. Errors by Spanish batteries.

CIVILIAN. Why by Spanish batteries?

GENERAL. Spanish batteries are not so good as ours.

[*The* CIVILIAN *does not answer and the firing keeps up although the batteries are not firing with the speed with which they commenced. There is an incoming whistling rush, then a roar, and a shell has landed just short of the observation post*]

GENERAL. They answer now a little.

[*There are no lights in the observation post now except that of the gun flashes and the light of the cigarette the* SENTRY *at the foot of the ladder is smoking. As you watch you see the glow of this cigarette describe half an arc in the dark, and there is a thud clearly heard by the audience as the* SENTRY *falls. You hear the sound of two blows. Another shell comes in with the same sort of screaming rush, and at its burst you see in the flash two men climbing the ladder*]

GENERAL. [*Speaking from the telemeter*] Ring me Garabitas.

[SIGNALLER *rings. Then rings again*]

SIGNALLER. Sorry, sir. The wire's gone.
GENERAL. [*To the other* SIGNALLER] Get me through to the Division.
SIGNALLER. I have no wire, sir.
GENERAL. Put some one to trace your wire!
SIGNALLER. Yes, sir.

[*He rises in the dark*]

GENERAL. What's that man smoking for? What sort of an army out of the chorus of *Carmen* is this?

[*You see the cigarette in the mouth of the* SENTRY *at the top of the ladder describe a long parabola toward the ground as though he had tossed it away, and there is the solid noise of a body falling. A flashlight illuminates the three men by the telemeters and the two* SIGNALLERS]

PHILIP. [*From inside the open door at the top of the ladder. In a low, very quiet voice*] Put your hands up and don't try anything heroic, or I'll blow your heads off!

[*He is holding a short automatic rifle which was slung over his back as he climbed up the ladder*]

I mean all five of you! *KEEP* them up there, you fat bastard!

[MAX *has a hand grenade in his right hand, the flashlight in his left*]

MAX. You make a noise, you move, and everybody is dead. You hear?

PHILIP. Who do you want?

MAX. Only the fat one and the townsman. Tie me up the rest. You have also good adhesive tape?

PHILIP. *Da.*

MAX. You see. We are all Russians. Everybody is Russians in Madrid! Hurry up, Tovarich, and tape good the mouths, because I have to throw this thing before we go. You see the pin is pulled already!

[*Just before the curtain goes down, as* PHILIP *is advancing toward them with the short automatic rifle, you see the men's white faces in the flashlight. The batteries are still firing. From below and beyond the house comes a voice—* "Cut out that light!"]

MAX. O.K. soldier, in just a minute!

CURTAIN

ACT THREE • SCENE THREE

As the curtain rises you see the same room in Seguridad headquarters that was shown in Act II, Scene I. ANTONIO, *of the Comisariato de Vigilan-*

cia, is sitting behind the table. PHILIP *and* MAX, *muddy and much the worse for wear, are seated in the two chairs.* PHILIP *still has the automatic rifle slung over his back. The* CIVILIAN *from the observation post, his beret gone, his trench coat ripped clean up the back, one sleeve hanging loose, is standing before the table with an* ASSAULT GUARD *on either side of him.*

ANTONIO. [*To the two* ASSAULT GUARDS] You can go!

[*They salute and go out to the right, carrying their rifles at trail*]
[*To* PHILIP]

What became of the other?

PHILIP. We lost him coming in.

MAX. He was too heavy and he would not walk.

ANTONIO. It would have been a wonderful capture.

PHILIP. You can't do these things as they do them in the cinema.

ANTONIO. Still, if we could have had him!

PHILIP. I'll draw you a little map and you can send out there and find him.

ANTONIO. Yes?

MAX. He was a soldier and he would never have talked. I would have liked the questioning of him, but such a business is useless.

PHILIP. When we're through here I'll draw you a little map and you can send out for him. No one will have moved him. We left him in a likely spot.

CIVILIAN. [*In an hysterical voice*] You *murdered* him.

PHILIP. [*Contemptuously*] Shut up, will you?

MAX. I promise you, he would not have ever talked. I know such men.

PHILIP. You see, we didn't expect to find two of these sportsmen at the same time. And this other specimen was oversized and he wouldn't walk finally. He made a sort of sit-down strike. And I don't know whether you've ever tried coming in at night from up there. There are a couple of very odd spots. So you see we didn't really have any bloody choice in the matter.

CIVILIAN. [*Hysterically*] So you murdered him! I saw you do it.

PHILIP. Just quiet down, will you? No one asked you for your opinion.

MAX. You want us now?

ANTONIO. No.

MAX. I think I like to go. This isn't what I like very much. It makes too much remember.

PHILIP. You need me?

ANTONIO. No.

PHILIP. You don't need to worry. You'll get everything—the lists, the locations, everything. This thing has been running it.

ANTONIO. Yes.

PHILIP. You don't need to worry about his talking. He's the talkative type.

ANTONIO. He is a politician. Yes. I have talked to many politicians.

CIVILIAN. [*Hysterically*] You'll never make me talk! Never! Never! Never!

[MAX *and* PHILIP *look at each other—*PHILIP *grins*]

PHILIP. [*Very quietly*] You're talking now. Haven't you noticed it?

CIVILIAN. No! No!

MAX. If it is all right I will go.

[*He stands up*]

PHILIP. I'll run along too, I think.

ANTONIO. You do not want to stay to hear it?

MAX. Please, no.

ANTONIO. It will be very interesting.

PHILIP. It's that we are tired.

ANTONIO. It will be very interesting.

PHILIP. I'll be by tomorrow.

ANTONIO. I would like you very much to stay.

MAX. Please. If you do not mind. As a favor.

CIVILIAN. What are you going to do to me?

ANTONIO. Nothing. Only that you should answer some questions.

CIVILIAN. I'll never talk.

ANTONIO. Oh, yes, you will!

MAX. Please. Please. I go now!

CURTAIN

ACT THREE • SCENE FOUR

Same as Act I, Scene III, but it is late afternoon. As the curtain rises, you see the two rooms. DOROTHY BRIDGES' *room is dark.* PHILIP'S *is lighted, with the curtains drawn.* PHILIP *is lying face down on the bed.* ANITA *is sitting on a chair by the bed.*

ANITA. Philip!

PHILIP. [*Not turning or looking toward her*] What's the matter?

ANITA. Please, Philip.

PHILIP. Please bloody what?

ANITA. Where is whiskey?

PHILIP. Under the bed.

ANITA. Thank you.

[*She looks under the bed. Then crawls part way under*]

No find.

PHILIP. Try the closet then. Somebody's been in here cleaning up again.

ANITA. [*Goes to the closet and opens it. She looks carefully inside*] Is all empty bottles.

PHILIP. You're just a little discoverer. Come here.

ANITA. I want find a whiskey.

PHILIP. Look in the night table.

[ANITA *goes over to the night table by the bed and opens the door—she brings out a bottle of whiskey. Goes for a glass into the bathroom, and pours a whiskey into it and adds water from the carafe by the bed*]

ANITA. Philip. Drink this feel better.

[PHILIP *sits up and looks at her*]

PHILIP. Hello, Black Beauty. How did you get in here?

ANITA. From the pass key.

PHILIP. Well.

ANITA. I no see you. I plenty worried. I come here they say you inside. I knock door no answer. I knock more. No answer. I say open me up with the pass key.

PHILIP. And they did?

ANITA. I said you sent for me.

PHILIP. Did I?

ANITA. No.

PHILIP. Thoughtful of you to come though.

ANITA. Philip you still that big blonde?

PHILIP. I don't know. I'm sort of mixed up about that. Things are getting sort of complicated. Every night I ask her to marry me, and every morning I tell her I don't mean it. I think, probably, things can't go on like that. No. They can't go on like that.

[ANITA *sits down by him and pats his head and smooths his hair back*]

ANITA. You feel plenty bad. I know.

PHILIP. Want me to tell you a secret?

ANITA. Yes.

PHILIP. I never felt worse.

ANITA. Is a disappoint. Was think you tell how you catch all the people of the Fifth Column.

PHILIP. I didn't catch them. Only caught one man. Disgusting specimen he was, too.

[*There is a knock on the door. It is the* MANAGER]

MANAGER. Excuse profoundly if disturbation——

PHILIP. Keep it clean you know. There's ladies present.

MANAGER. I mean only to enter and see if every *thing* in order. Control possible actions of young lady in case your absence or incapacity. Also desire offer sincerest warmest greetings congratulations admirable performance feat of counterespionage resulting announcement evening papers arrest three hundred members Fifth Column.

PHILIP. That's in the paper?

MANAGER. With details of arrestations of every type of reprehensible engaged in shooting, plotting assassinations—sabotaging, communicating with enemy, every form of delights.

PHILIP. Of delights?

MANAGER. Is a French word, spells out D-E-L-I-T-S, meaning offenses.

PHILIP. And that's all in the paper?

MANAGER. Absolutely, Mr. Philip.

PHILIP. And where do I come in?

MANAGER. Oh, everybody knows you were engaged in prosecution of such investigations.

PHILIP. Just how do they know?

MANAGER. [*Reproachfully*] Mr. Philip. Is Madrid. In Madrid everybody knows everything often before occurrence of same. After occurrence sometimes is discussions as to who actually did. But before occurrence all the world knows clearly who must do. I offer congratulations now in order to precede reproaches of unsatisfiables who ask, "Ah ha! Only 300? Where are the others?"

PHILIP. Don't be so gloomy. I suppose I'll have to be leaving now though.

MANAGER. Mr. Philip, I have thought of that and I come here, make what hope will result as excellent proposition. If you leave is useless to carry tinned goods as baggage.

[*There is a knock on the door. It is* MAX]

MAX. Salud Camaradas.

EVERY ONE. Salud.

PHILIP. [*To* MANAGER] Run along now, Comrade Stamp Collector. We can talk about that later.

MAX. [*To* PHILIP] *Wie gehts?*

PHILIP. *Gut.* Not too *gut.*

ANITA. O.K. I take bath?

PHILIP. More than O.K., darling. But keep the door shut, will you?

ANITA. [*From bathroom*] Is warm water.

PHILIP. That's a good sign. Shut the door, please.

> [ANITA *shuts the door.* MAX *comes over by the bed and sits down on a chair.* PHILIP *is sitting on the bed with his legs hanging over*]

PHILIP. Want anything?

MAX. No, Comrade. You were there?

PHILIP. Oh, yes. I stayed all through it. Every bit of it. All of it. They needed to know something and they called me back.

MAX. How was he?

PHILIP. Cowardly. But it only came out a little at a time for a while.

MAX. And then?

PHILIP. Oh, and then finally he was spilling it out faster than a stenographer could take it. I have a strong stomach, you know.

MAX. [*Ignoring this*] I see in the paper about the arrests. Why do they publish such things?

PHILIP. I don't know, my boy. Why do they? I'll bite.

MAX. It is good for morale. But it is also very good to get every one. Did they bring in—the—ah——

PHILIP. Oh, yes. The corpse you mean? They fetched him in from where we left him, and Antonio had him placed in a chair in the corner and I put a cigarette in his mouth and lit it and it was all very jolly. Only the cigarette wouldn't stay lighted, of course.

MAX. I am very happy I did not have to stay.

PHILIP. I stayed. And then I left. And then I came back. Then

I left and they called me back again. I've been there until an hour ago and now I'm through. For today, that is. Finished my work for the day. Something else to do tomorrow.

MAX. We did very good job.

PHILIP. As good as we could. It was very brilliant and very flashy, and there were probably many holes in the net and a big part of the haul got away. But they can haul again. You have to send me some place else though. I'm no good here any more. Too many people know what I'm doing. *Not* because I talk, either. It just gets that way.

MAX. There are many places to send. But you still have some work to do here.

PHILIP. I know. But ship me out as quickly as you can, will you? I'm getting on the jumpy side.

MAX. What about the girl in the other room?

PHILIP. Oh, I'm going to break it off with her.

MAX. I do not ask that.

PHILIP. No. But you would sooner or later. There's no sense babying me along. We're in for fifty years of undeclared wars and I've signed up for the duration. I don't exactly remember when it was, but I signed up all right.

MAX. So have we all. There is no question of signing. There is no need to talk with bitterness.

PHILIP. I'm not bitter. I just don't want to fool myself. Nor let things get a hold in part of me where no things should get hold. This thing was getting pretty well in. Well, I know how to cure it.

MAX. How?

PHILIP. I'll show you how.

MAX. Remember, Philip, I am a kind man.

PHILIP. Oh, quite. So am I. You ought to watch me work sometime.

[*While they have been talking you see the door of 109 open and* DOROTHY BRIDGES *comes in. She turns up the lights, takes off her street coat and puts on the silver fox cape. Standing, she turns in it before the mirror. She looks very beautiful this evening. She goes to the phonograph and puts on the Chopin Mazurka and sits in a chair by the reading light with a book]*

PHILIP. There she is. She's come, what do you call the place, home—now.

MAX. Philip, Comrade, you do not have to. I tell you truly I see no signs that she interferes with your work in any way.

PHILIP. No, but I do. And you would damned soon.

MAX. I leave it to you as before. But remember to be kind. To us to whom dreadful things have been done, kindness in all *possible* things is of great importance.

PHILIP. I'm very kind, too, you know. Oh, am I kind! I'm terrific!

MAX. No, I do not know that you are kind. I would like you to be.

PHILIP. Just wait in here, will you?

[PHILIP *goes out of the door and knocks on the door of 109. He pushes it open after knocking and goes in]*

DOROTHY. Hello, beloved.

PHILIP. Hello. How have you been?

DOROTHY. I'm very well and very happy now you're here. Where have you been? You never came in last night. Oh, I'm so *glad* you're here.

PHILIP. Have you a drink?

DOROTHY. Yes, darling.

[*She makes him a whiskey and water. In the other room* MAX *is sitting in a chair staring at the electric stove]*

DOROTHY. Where were you, Philip?

PHILIP. Just around. Checking up on things.

DOROTHY. And how were things?

PHILIP. Some were good, you know. And some were not so good. I suppose they evened up.

DOROTHY. And you don't have to go out tonight?

PHILIP. I don't know.

DOROTHY. Philip, beloved, what's the matter?

PHILIP. Nothing's the matter.

DOROTHY. Philip, let's go away from here. I don't have to stay here. I've sent away three articles. We could go to that place near Saint-Tropez and the rains haven't started yet and it would be lovely there now with no people. Then afterwards we could go to ski.

PHILIP. [*Very bitterly*] Yes, and afterwards to Egypt and make love happily in all the hotels, and a thousand breakfasts come up on trays in the thousand fine mornings of the next three years; or the ninety of the next three months; or however long it took you to be tired of me, or me of you. And all we'd do would be amuse ourselves. We'd stay at the Crillon, or the Ritz, and in the fall when the leaves were off the trees in the Bois and it was sharp and cold, we'd drive out to Auteuil steeplechasing, and keep warm by those big coal braziers in the paddock, and watch them take the water jump and see them coming over the bullfinch and the old stone wall. That's it. And nip into the bar for a champagne cocktail and afterwards ride back in to dinner at La Rue's and weekends go to shoot pheasants in the Sologne. Yes, yes, that's it. And fly out to Nairobi and the old Mathaiga Club, and in the spring a little spot of salmon fishing. Yes, yes, that's it. And every night in bed together. Is that it?

DOROTHY. Oh, darling, think how it would be! Have you *that* much money?

PHILIP. I did have. Till I got into this business.

DOROTHY. And we'll do all that and Saint Moritz, too?

PHILIP. Saint Moritz? Don't be vulgar. Kitzbühel you mean. You meet people like Michael Arlen at Saint Moritz.

DOROTHY. But you wouldn't have to meet him, darling. You could cut him. And will we really do all that?

PHILIP. Do you want to?

DOROTHY. Oh, darling!

PHILIP. Would you like to go to Hungary, too, some fall? You can take an estate there very cheaply and only pay for what you shoot. And on the Danube flats you have great flights of geese. And have you ever been to Lamu where the long white beach is, with the dhows beached on their sides, and the wind in the palms at night? Or what about Malindi where you can surfboard on the beach and the northeast monsoon cool and fresh, and no pajamas, and no sheets at night. You'd like Malindi.

DOROTHY. I know I would, Philip.

PHILIP. And have you ever been out to the Sans Souci in Havana on a Saturday night to dance in the Patio under the royal palms? They're gray and they rise like columns and you stay up all night there and play dice, or the wheel, and drive in to Jaimanitas for breakfast in the daylight. And everybody knows every one else and it's very pleasant and gay.

DOROTHY. Can we go there?

PHILIP. No.

DOROTHY. Why not, Philip?

PHILIP. We won't go anywhere.

DOROTHY. Why not, darling?

PHILIP. You can go if you like. I'll draw you up an itinerary.

DOROTHY. But why can't we go together?

PHILIP. You can go. But I've been to all those places and I've left them all behind. And where I go now I go alone, or with others who go there for the same reason I go.

DOROTHY. And I can't go there?

PHILIP. No.

DOROTHY. And why can't I go wherever it is? I could learn and I'm *not* afraid.

PHILIP. One reason is I don't know where it is. And another is I wouldn't take you.

DOROTHY. Why not?

PHILIP. Because you're useless, really. You're uneducated, you're useless, you're a fool and you're lazy.

DOROTHY. Maybe the others. But I'm not useless.

PHILIP. Why aren't you useless?

DOROTHY. You know—or you ought to know.

[*She is crying*]

PHILIP. Oh, yes. *That.*

DOROTHY. Is that all it means to you?

PHILIP. That's a commodity you shouldn't pay too high a price for.

DOROTHY. So I'm a commodity?

PHILIP. Yes, a very handsome commodity. The most beautiful I ever had.

DOROTHY. Good. I'm glad to hear you say it. And I'm glad it's daylight. Now get out of here. You conceited, *conceited* drunkard. You ridiculous, puffed-up, posing braggart. You commodity, you. Did it ever occur to you that you're a commodity, too? A commodity one shouldn't pay too high a price for?

PHILIP. [*Laughing*] No. But I see it the way you put it.

DOROTHY. Well, you are. You're a perfectly vicious commodity. Never home. Out all night. Dirty, muddy, disorderly. You're a *terrible* commodity. I just liked the package it was put up in. That was all. I'm glad you're going away.

PHILIP. Really?

DOROTHY. Yes, *really.* You and your commodity. But you didn't have to mention all those places if we weren't ever going to them.

PHILIP. I'm very sorry. That wasn't kind.

DOROTHY. Oh, don't be kind either. You're frightful when you're kind. Only kind people should try being kind. You're horrible when you're kind. And you didn't have to mention them in the daytime.

PHILIP. I'm sorry.

DOROTHY. Oh, don't be sorry. You're at your *worst* when you're sorry. I can't *stand* you sorry. Just get out.

PHILIP. Well, good-bye.

[*He puts his arms around her to kiss her*]

DOROTHY. Don't kiss me either. You'll kiss me and then you'll go right in to commodities. I know you.

[PHILIP *holds her tight and kisses her*]

Oh, Philip, Philip, Philip.

PHILIP. Good-bye.

DOROTHY. You—you—you don't want the commodity?

PHILIP. I can't afford it.

[DOROTHY *twists away from him*]

DOROTHY. Then, go then.

PHILIP. Good-bye.

DOROTHY. Oh, get out.

[PHILIP *goes out the door and into his room.* MAX *is still sitting in the chair. In the other room* DOROTHY *rings the bell for the maid*]

MAX. So?

[PHILIP *stands there looking into the electric stove.* MAX *looks into the stove too. In the other room* PETRA *has come to the door*]

PETRA. Yes, Señorita.

[DOROTHY *is sitting on the bed. Her head is up but there are tears running down her cheeks.* PETRA *goes over to her*]

What is it, Señorita?

DOROTHY. Oh, Petra, he's bad just as you said he was. He's bad, bad, bad. And like a damn fool I thought we were going to be happy. But he's bad.

PETRA. Yes, Señorita.

DOROTHY. But oh, Petra, the trouble is I *love* him.

[PETRA *stands there by the bed with* DOROTHY. *In Room 110* PHILIP *stands in front of the night table. He pours himself a whiskey and puts water in it*]

PHILIP. Anita.

ANITA. [*From inside the bathroom*] Yes, Philip.

PHILIP. Anita, come out whenever you've finished your bath.

MAX. I go.

PHILIP. No. Stay around.

MAX. No. No. No. Please, I go.

PHILIP. [*In a very dry flat voice*] Anita, was the water hot?

ANITA. [*From inside the bathroom*] Was lovely bath.

MAX. I go. Please, please, please, I go.

CURTAIN